DOLPHIN GIRL

Scott Neil

Elvin Books

BERMUDA

IMPORTANT NOTICE:

READER'S RESOURCE: Scottish and slang words
To maintain the Scottish authenticity and flavour of this novel, a small number of Scottish words and slang phrases will be found dotted throughout the novel.
To assist readers who are unfamiliar with these words, an alphabetical list with definitions can be found at the back of this book.
Appendix: Dictionary of Scottish and slang words

Elvin Books, Bermuda
www.scottneilauthor.com

Publisher's Note: This is a work of fiction. Names, characters, places, and incidents are a product of the author's imagination. Locales and public names are sometimes used for atmospheric purposes. Any resemblance to actual people, living or dead, or to businesses, companies, events, institutions, or locales is completely coincidental.

Cover Design: **Kit Foster**
Book Layout © 2014 BookDesignTemplates.com

Dolphin Girl/ Scott Neil -- 1st edition
ISBN 978-1-927750-85-8 (paperback)
ISBN 978-1-927750-86-3 (ebook)

For Heather

Surrealism to me is reality

—JOHN LENNON

CONTENTS

CHAPTER ONE

25 YEARS AGO

"You'll burn your eyes out."

"Who will?"

"You will. Staring at the sun."

"I'm no staring at the sun." Katrina scanned the sky, her raised left arm shielding the glare of the mid-afternoon sun, the blouse sleeve billowing gently in the breeze. Swirling jet-black hair spiralled carelessly around her head, the dancing twists of demented snakes cloaking deep green eyes.

Her slender frame barely concealed the rhythmic rise and fall of her chest as she breathed in step with the estuary's tide. Taller than most girls in high school first year, Katrina was thin, though not excruciatingly. Her features were those of an elf. Her chin a little too small, her mouth a fraction too wide and her gently upturned nose overpowered by green saucer eyes.

Tantalisingly revealed by the half open blouse collar Josh spied the baby soft skin at the nape of her neck glowing golden with the first tinge of May sunshine.

"Then what are you looking at?" he asked, dropping his leather satchel on the beach and popping a fruit drop into his mouth. It was pear flavoured, but already the salt impregnated air of the River Forth bit at his lips. He didn't care for it much. He didn't care for school much either. That was where he and Katrina should have been, but they always bunked off on Tuesday afternoons and Thursday mornings. As for Friday afternoons – well, Josh couldn't believe anyone was seriously expected to go to school with the weekend close enough to smell.

Eleven summers had passed since his mother had been rushed to hospital to give birth. She almost died. Josh treated the story as tittle-tattle designed to instill some sense of gratitude. The self-styled hard man of Craigmuir School wasn't known for caring much about anything.

But then there was gypsy-esque Katrina. An elf out of time. Did he care for her? He was momentarily hypnotised by the seaweed coils of black hair tossed around her pretty head.

"Look!" Katrina's excited voice jumped an octave. She pointed across the sea, "Through the broken clouds the shafts of sunlight striking the water without so much as a splash."

Josh grunted.

"Doesn't it make you feel insignificant, like an ant on a Cezanne?"

"Eh?" Josh glanced sideways. He wasn't what girls termed 'a looker'. Chubby baby fat still clung to his cheeks, weakening the impact of his cultivated sneer. His brown, greasy mop of hair an upturned bowl hiding thick eyebrows and shading narrow hazel eyes that peered from a near-perfect oval face. The inch or two in height he surrendered to his peers was made up for in bare-faced attitude.

Yet Katrina glimpsed the handsome, mature man Josh would one day become, able to appreciate the finer things in life. She must be patient.

Distant, almost inaudible laughter distracted her.

"What are they doing?" Katrina pointed to the water's edge where the sweeping estuary that was the Firth of Forth had retreated to its furthest point to roll playfully along the flat sand. Josh followed her slender digit and saw three figures kicking at a shape lying on the ground.

"Dunno. Let's go find out." He retrieved his leather satchel and slung it over his blazer's ripped sleeve. Katrina slipped her arm under his.

"What are you missing?"

"Maths, with Mr Boot. The loser," Josh popped another fruit drop into his mouth - apple. He offered Katrina one. She took a cherry drop from the crumpled paper bag.

"I'm supposed to be in PE," she said. "There's no way I'm doing another silly cross country run in the freezing cold. I told Miss Shipley I had a dentist's appointment. Again." She tightened her hold on Josh's arm. Laughter swathed them. Then there was silence as they trudged, Katrina focusing on the damp sand clinging to her buckled black shoes, Josh delighting in dragging his feet and scuffing his shoes with each step.

"What are you going to do when you leave school?" Katrina was solemn.

Josh stopped walking, glanced over his shoulder and pointed at the triple-bellied steel behemoth behind them. The Forth Bridge had a bold and majestic presence, spanning the waters of the firth and carrying trains to the distant shore of Fife and beyond.

"I'm gonna be a painter on that," Josh boasted proudly and started dragging his feet again. A furrow trailed behind him next to Katrina's soft footprints.

"What do you wannae to do that fur?" Katrina asked.

"Job for life, innit. Soon as you've finished you have to go back to the start and do it all again."

"I dinnae want a husband who paints bridges for a living."

"What do you want me to do then?"

"A fireman, or a prime minister. And I wouldn't be interested if you smoked or boozed."

Josh met her eyes. "I'll never smoke and I'll never be an alkay. I've seen what it has done to ma faither." His steps quickened. Katrina trotted to keep up, her eyes fixed on his dark brown hair shifting from side to side along his broad shoulders, caught by the breeze, swaying in time with his body.

"I thought your parents split up?"

"Aye, but I still see my faither doon the toon staggering about, steaming. I'll never be like him. Waster."

Now they were near enough to see that the figures on the beach were boys, perhaps a year or two older, skipping school just like them. All three abruptly turned. There were no smiles.

"What do you want?" asked the first.

"What are you kicking?" Josh's casual veneer held fast.

"Nowt to do with you. Fuck off."

"That's a dolphin!" Katrina's eyes widened, focusing on the object at the boys' feet.

The second youth stepped forward. There was a visible scar, carved with the precision of a knife blade, running from the corner of his left eye to the side of his mouth. "Yer, and it's almost deed. We're putting it oot of its misery. And we'll do the same to youse if you don't bugger off."

Josh flicked his eyes to Katrina and flinched his head backwards. It was time to go. She stared back, wasn't he going to stop them? Ignoring her silent, pleading eyes he grabbed her forearm, forcibly marching her away across the wet sand.

"Josh!"

"Wheesht, I know what I'm doing."

Once downwind and out of listening range he stopped.

"Josh, we can't let…." Katrina started to protest, Josh nudged her.

"Ssssh, listen. Here's what we're gonna do. I'll go back up and distract them, get them to chase me across the beach. As soon as they start running after me, you get up there and shove the fish back in the water," he instructed.

At first the three boys didn't see Josh return. They were preoccupied laying the boot into the dolphin.

"You still fucking here?" said the first boy, noticing Josh standing beside him. The boys stopped kicking. "I thought we told you to clear off."

Josh cracked a smile. "So you did. But I was jist wondering what a bunch of gaylords like youse were daein on the beach together." He reached down and grabbed one of the boys' PVC sports bags from the sand. Then he was gone, fleeing along the beach with the stolen bag slung over his shoulder, puffing cool air, heading in the opposite direction to where he had left Katrina,

"Bastard, come back wae that!"

Josh didn't know which one of the boys had called out. He didn't look back. He knew they were chasing, he could hear wheezing voices and the dull thud of shoes on wet sand. He picked up his knees forcing himself faster until the horizon was a jiggling blur.

Katrina seized the moment. Like a sneak thief she approached the stricken dolphin, its skin a glistening mixture of seawater and blood. She leaned forward and touched it. There was a reaction – it was still alive. Dark almond-shaped eyes pleading looked upwards. An unspoken message was transmitted. With both hands Katrina pushed the dolphin, forcing it closer to the water's edge. The tide was turning. Water lapped against the beached creature. Katrina prayed and pushed, at last the dolphin slid deep enough into the water to gain flotation.

"Go, go!" she urged and the dolphin responded. Its flippers flicked, it turned its head from the sand to the open water and in a moment its dark shape had slipped away until only the tip of its dorsal fin was visible. Then it was gone. Exhilaration gripped Katrina. She turned, searching for Josh.

Josh could feel his legs tiring as lactic acid started to build up, but he still had a healthy gap between himself and his pursuers. He turned in a wide arc, catching the boys unaware as he doubled-back. His shoes slapped against the wet sand at the water's edge. His vision was blurred from the headlong running, but he could see the distant figure of Katrina ahead of him.

"Run Katrina, run!"

She needed no encouraging and ran in the direction he was heading. Soon Josh was up on her shoulder. Behind they heard shouts of enraged indignation. Between laboured breaths Josh squeezed out laughter. He glanced back. "They've stopped running. They've given up." He fell to his knees laughing.

TWO SUMMERS LATER

"Shouldn't you be at school?" Wally MacPherson liked to state the bleeding obvious. Josh knew it was a mistake going into Wally's cornershop because it was the hub of the neighbourhood gossip and news that he'd been clocked skiving at two in the afternoon would reach home before he did. He shrugged at Wally's question and played dumb.

"You'll no make any'hing out of your life if you don't study the books. Take it from me," Wally lectured as he turned away and reached up to the second highest shelf to grab the plastic jar of fruit drops. Sure, Wally was one to talk, he was a prime example of what a hard working youngster could look forward to later in life – working all day in a poxy cornershop on the edge of the most shite housing scheme in Edinburgh. Stuff your books where the sun disnae shine, Wally. Of course Josh said none of this out loud, for the thoughts of a 14-year-old would not be welcomed on the premises, besides which, it was unwise to upset Wally when there was a chance that 'keeping it zipped' might bring a few extra fruit drops above and beyond the ordered quarter pound. The jar tipped over a set of shiny scales and Josh watched the cascade of sugary treats pile up. The moment the hand of the scales pointed to a quarter, the waterfall of fruit drops abruptly stopped.

"A quarter you said?" Wally checked.

"Aye," Josh nodded, straining to see if one more fruit drop would slide from the jar. A further seven tumbled onto the dish before the lid was twisted back on and the jar replaced on the shelf beside the widest range of sweets available outside the city centre. Nice one Wally, Josh thought to himself as he fumbled in his pocket for change and placed three ten pence coins on top of the Prime Minister's head, which looked out from the front cover of the Daily Record newspaper resting on the counter.

"I hope that's no your dinner money you've gied me. You've got to eat properly if you want to be a big, strong healthy fella," Wally chided as he took the coins. Josh grabbed the paper poke of sweets and marched quickly from the shop. Outside, and just around the corner from the shop window so she would not been seen, Katrina was waiting. She had daisies in her hand and had made a short chain, which she now swung gently as she walked beside Josh.

From Wally's shop it is a short stroll to the jetty, which led to the beach at Cramond. It was a favourite skiving hang out that had lately become more dangerous as teachers from a number of schools were now wise to the hideout and the would-be spies carried out regular patrols.

Josh knew plenty of hidden enclaves and dunes where he and Katrina could hunker down in splendid isolation for a few hours before heading home. As far as he was concerned a double session of afternoon maths made it no contest between Cramond and Craigmuir School. The shine on his brown shoes had lasted for one day of the new school term. Four weeks later they had been scuffed beyond recognition, scarred by the trials of playground football and climbing the fence behind the science block to secure afternoons away at the beach. The shoe leather was now being ground away further as fine grains of sand rolled across them. Josh stopped walking, dropped his satchel on the sand and took another fruit drop. It was pear-flavoured. A refreshing sea breeze tugged at Katrina's coiled black hair as she launched her half-made daisy chain into the wind. There was almost enough of an updraft for it to fly. Almost. It fell to the ground a few feet away. But the daisy chain was of no consequence anymore. She sensed something wasn't right.

Josh picked up his satchel, hitched it on his right shoulder and loosened his school tie. Katrina grabbed his left arm. "This is where we helped the dolphin," she pointed to the wave-stroked sand, remembering the moment from two years before. Josh grunted.

"It is! I know it is," Katrina's enthusiasm remained unpunctured. "It must be out there somewhere with all its friends, in a big huddle or something. What do you call a group of dolphins?" She released his arm and gazed across the watery miles of the estuary, waiting for a reply that did not come. "It's not a pack or a swarm...what do you think it's called?" she asked again.

"A dream," Josh sighed.

"A dream of dolphins. Wow, what a beautiful name, Josh....Josh." Josh was away, heading for distant sand dunes. Katrina gave chase, calling his name. For the next five minutes she mixed and matched the same three words. "Josh, what's wrong?" She tried again. First she asked him to speak, then she asked him if he wasn't speaking, then finally why wasn't he speaking. The stony silence remained until he flung himself into the natural bowl of a sand dune. Katrina dropped her school bag and fell to her knees by his side. She tugged his right arm until finally he spoke.

"When did you find out?" he asked.

Katrina took a moment. "Last week. I didnae know how to tell you."

There was a pause.

"Is it definite?"

"Aye," Katrina dropped her head. "I'm sorry Josh." She stood up, brushing sand from her knees and grey skirt and climbing to the rim of the sand dune to peer at the distant shoreline. A salt-laden wind streamed against her hair. A few moments passed before she sensed Josh beside her. "It doesn't have to be the end, Josh."

"How?"

"I'll...I'll come back visiting."

"All the way from Oxford? How far's that? Hundreds of miles."

Katrina caught a tear and rubbed it away. "It's all ma faither's fault. I dinnae ken why he couldn't get a job here. He keeps saying Scotland's finished and there's no work. He just disnae look fur it in the right places."

"Well, looks like I'll be skipping school on ma own. It'll no be the same without you," Josh huffed.

"I'll come back. When I've finished ma studies I'll come back to Edinburgh and we'll have our own hoose. You wait fur me and I'll wait fur you. Is it a deal?"

"How long?" Josh met her eyes.

"No long. A few years."

"What two, four? You go to university or something and I'll no see you 'till you're in your twenties."

There was an uneasy silence.

"Am I no worth the wait?" A tear trickled down her left cheek. Josh kissed it away.

"It's a deal then. You wait for me and I'll wait for you?" Katrina offered her hand. Josh shook it.

"Deal."

Katrina smiled. "You better no run off way anyone else. Anyway, I know where to find you when I come back."

"Oh aye, where?"

"Over there painting that again and again," she laughed, pointing at the Forth Bridge.

CHAPTER THREE

FOUR MONTHS AGO

Katrina had initially stayed prominent in Josh's thoughts, but as the years went by without any contact his memory of her faded until she was just another melancholy–drizzled relic of his youth. He was now in his 30s, scarred by life's battles and stripped of the hallucination of invincibility he'd had as the boy on the beach.

It was night and he drunkenly staggered along a street. He tried to re-orientate. His glazed eyes fixed on guttering rainwater cascading through a roadside drain. African man gazed at the star-sprinkled heavens and said nothing.

"Just you keep it shut." Josh's menacing but unnecessary threat tripped over a hiccup. African man's smile never twitched and his eyes portrayed the weary expression of one who had seen it all before and had wisdom enough not to pass comment. Rainwater dragged at Josh's jeans as he propped himself against African man's shoulder.

"That wis your fault for being so heavy," he admonished, dimly flicking his eyes along the wet pavement.

The rain had stopped and the guilty clouds, blown hither by a chilly breeze, let in the blinking eyes of stars to crown this forgotten corner of the world, this forgotten corner of Scotland.

This was Edinburgh, but as far removed from the touristy grandeur of the city centre as possible. This was the Bain housing estate. To be exact this was Monkland Road. The last stragglers of the night ghosted past in the shadows, hardly stopping to glance, too wrapped up in their chip paper wrappings.

"You're all bastards!" Josh directed his words at the world and anyone lurking ahead for an easy mugging. He figured there would be at least one chancer.

"There's two of us. Lay a finger and you'll no live to regret it!" There was no reply from the imagined assailants of the night. Josh hiccupped and gripped African man around the waist, lifting and turning him under arm.

"And why you can't walk yourself, I don't know. Dinnae drink a drop all night and I've got to carry you all the way home. Do I look stupid or something?"

As a car passed Josh brushed into a hedgerow, the rain-soaked leaves dowsed him in water. "Don't worry about me. I'll jist walk hame if it's all the same to you," he yelled at the departing taillights.

Worn shoe heels clicked an absurd and unjolly rhythm. A loose shoelace dragged. So late, and after imbibing more than his fill of 'heavy' at The Gannet public house, he now relied on an inbuilt sixth sense to guide his way home – the unfailing automatic pilot of every steaming drinker.

"I'm bursting."

African man stood on his own as Josh released a steaming arc through a wire mesh fence. Beyond the fence were the ghastly remains of the iron forge works where four hundred men had once toiled. The wind whistling through the wire spoke of the workers' laughing chatter before they had all been made redundant and dumped on the dole.

Josh spat through the mesh. "Take all our jobs away and leave us with nowt!" He zipped his flies and turned to African man. "You don't know how lucky you are not to have seen what they did to us."

A church bell chimed three as Josh, with African man tucked under his arm, reached the rundown council scheme. Familiar graffiti, boarded up windows, and a kerbside peppered with burnt out rusting husks of cars told him he was home.

African man nutted the front door.

"Shush, there's nae need for that," Josh fumbled for his keys as he castigated his silent companion. At the fifth attempt the lock turned and African man was carried over the threshold. Not daring to switch on a light, Josh fingered his way past the staircase to the living room where only the single red standby light of the television penetrated the darkness.

"Now you stay there and dinnae dare make a sound. If Suzy wakes up we'll both be oot on our arses." With his own warning ringing in his ears Josh slumped on to the leather settee, which groaned in a flatulent style. His ale-soaked breath was soon condensing against the smooth brown upholstery.

≈

Suzy had screamed before. Usually directly into Josh's face.

"What the fuck!" As stark morning light fought through the heavy living room curtains Suzy had been caught unaware. Not by the smell of stale beer and dim snoring of Josh comatose on the sofa, she had expected that. But a barely dressed, six-foot African tribesman staring through the gloom, that was another matter.

Josh jumped awake. "What...what's up?" He rubbed the piss holes in the snow that passed for his eyes. Frozen at the door, Suzy's hand covered her mouth.

"Och, it's only a statue. Have you no seen one afore?" Josh tried to reassure.

"Get it oot of this hoose. I'm not having weird crap like that in here." Suzy's words rang with finality.

"Suzy. It's an ornament. It brightens the place." But she was gone, her bare feet slapping on the linoleum.

"Aye, and it'll brighten up the garden when I set fire to it," she shouted back. Josh followed her to the kitchen. She refused to turn to face him.

"Och, don't start this. No the back treatment."

Suzy's back didn't answer.

"It was a bargain. Stovey sold it to me for fifty quid. See, if you want to buy one of these in the shops it'll cost four hundred...or mair."

The kettle was filled and banged hard on the worktop. Bread was rifled into the toaster.

"Come on, hen. It was a bargain. What was I supposed to do?"

"How about telling Stovey to shove it. Has it ever occurred to you that we don't have money to throw away on junk? I'm the only wan bringing money into this hoose." Suzy spun to face Josh, the taste of unspoken bitter words on her lips, eyes shrouded in black mascara. "When did you last do a stitch of work?"

"That's no fair. They shut the works doon and you ken I've been on the sick with my bad back."

Suzy nodded. "Aye, that's right. Cannae work for two years but you can go drinking every night while I'm slaving away to bring in some pin money." Clattering pots and unwashed dishes took the brunt of her anger. Josh got the back treatment again.

"Do you think I wouldn't be out working if I could? Because you're wrang, I loved working..."

"Don't come it, Josh. You're a no good layabout. My mother was right. I shouldnae have got involved with you in the first place. You've done bog all since we moved in."

The cutlery sang out of tune as Suzy dried them with a cloth and threw them into a drawer. The whistling kettle joined in, billowing steam into the heated atmosphere.

Josh backed off, seeking sanctuary in the living room. "And you can shut up," he warned African man as he confronted the carved wooden statue. He opened the curtains revealing another bleak day.

Four skiving kids in grey school trousers and matching jerseys kicked a ball along the empty road. They were the neighbourhood lads who rarely made it to school and instead guised around the allotments most days.

"Look at this shit hole." Suzy had returned, her hands cradled a cup of steaming tea. Josh's cup was empty and still hanging up in the kitchen cupboard, not that he needed to inquire. Suzy's anger was on the boil. "There's no a piece of furniture that matches. Nae carpet, faded curtains, a coffee table that's too low."

The coffee table was another purchase from Stovey. It was an oval, smoked glass affair, but stood at shin level making it an uncomfortable stretch to retrieve anything from. Suzy stared at African man. She had not mentioned the four breakfast barstools Josh brought from The Gannet last month. She had refused to even try to eat a meal sitting on the stools that were as high as the dining table. Josh waited for the stools to be dragged into the row, or the tiger-print wall carpet hanging menacingly above the settee.

"Everything you bring into this hoose is crap. Everything." Suzy swung her words at African man. The statue remained silent. She turned and looked contemptuously towards Josh then left the room.

Josh started to breathe again. Every day was the same. He flopped onto the settee, the hiss of air escaping from the upholstery as it moulded around him. Lying on his back he stared at the bare light bulb dangling from the ceiling. The spinning sensation that had dogged him since he left The Gannet at half-past two in the morning turned his swollen, gurgling stomach. He tried to recollect his tally of pints. Dipping a hand into the tight, front pocket of his jeans he pulled out a crumpled five-pound note, two one pound coins and some shrapnel. Forty quid had leaked away, not counting the fifty he now owed Stovey for African man. He groaned and stuffed the money back, farting with dismay.

The room swam. The wallpaper was discoloured by age and frayed and torn at the corners. The curtains were leftovers from previous occupants. In the hallway the letterbox rattled as something was pushed through. A few minutes passed then Suzy appeared, doing up a thick coat and throwing a brown envelope on to Josh's stomach. "There's your unemployment benefit. How long before you piss that up the wall?" she chided.

"Leave me alone. I'm no hurting anyone."

"No hurting anyone? I'm breaking ma back looking after this place while you slouch around and drink your benefit doon the boozer. No think you're hurting me?"

Josh's hungover cranial throbbed. "Every time I go out for a drink it's the same."

"Aye, which means it's the same six days a week." There was no pity to be found in Suzy's shrouded mascara black eyes.

"What dae I have to do to please you, eh?" Josh's words dripped sarcasm.

"You've got the cheek to ask?"

"Aye, I've got the cheek to ask. I bring things into the house. I cook meals."

"It's my wages from cleaning the bogs at the social that keep us afloat, no your beans on fucking toast," Suzy shot back.

Josh flicked the envelope on his chest. Suzy's contempt-filled eyes turned from him as she remembered the day they had moved in six years earlier. Josh had been working then. They had money for good furniture, money for going out, money for enjoying themselves. Then Josh crocked his back at the cement works lifting bags when the hoist broke – or so he claimed in order to secure a healthy sickness payment which now tidied him over. He had actually slipped and fallen over a pallet while "acting the goat" on the night shift. That was the tale Suzy overheard from Josh's mates in The Gannet, and Josh said nothing to contradict the claim, at least in the pub. Without his weekly wage coming in the payments on the furniture fell by the wayside and bailiffs arrived. The shame peaked when they got behind on the mortgage and everything of worth in the house that hadn't already been taken was sold or pawned.

Worse, in Suzy's eyes, was that "that cow" Lesley Craven had offered fifty quid for the shag pile living room carpet and Josh accepted it before telling her. When Josh's accident claim finally come through things got better for a few months as a portion of the cash found its way into the household money pot. But that had long gone by the board and now the cash was passed directly to Tom Tom, landlord of The Gannet.

As the morning sun reflected off the bare floorboards the hurt bubbled inside Suzy. "You're a waster, so you are, a waste of space. Have you no respect for the way you live, for the way I have to live?"

On his feet, arms on hips, Josh squared up to his common-law wife, "I bloody well bring things into this hoose. You jist dinnae appreciate any of them," he protested. His sudden movement sent the room tumbling at right angles, but he snorted and ignored his wonky vision.

"Is it any bloody surprise? What do I want with a carved dod o' wood?" Suzy replied.

"Ye see. You just don't get it." Josh folded his arms. "Tell me one thing that'll make you happy. Just one thing I can do that'll make you happy and I'll go and dae it."

Suzy matched his stance. She had heard it all before. "Magic up some carpet for this doss house."

"Carpet! Is that what you want? Is that what'll make you happy? Right."

Suzy swayed backwards as Josh finally did something she had not expected; he marched out of the front door.

CHAPTER FOUR

CARPET

"What about your benefit?" Suzy shouted.

Josh strode purposefully through the burned toast haze wafting from the windows of the crumbling housing estate.

"I dinnae need it," he replied, thrusting his hands in pockets, fumbling his seven pounds and 52 pence. His socks were still wet from last night's rain, which had soaked through the holes in his foundry boots. His feet squelched with every step. A blister throbbed on the tip of his right toe.

A skulking cloud blanket did its upmost to fill the off-grey estate with eternal gloom. It could hardly get more depressing. Then it did.

"Pissing rain," Josh addressed the heavens. The mizzle – an objectionably cross of mist and drizzle – started to permeate everything, stealthily soaking. The parade of shops near Ferrybridge was still a mile away. He felt the mizzle collect on the back of his neck and trickle downwards. Should have taken your coat, Josh could hear Suzy's lecture already. He brushed a hand through his hair forcing the water to run faster down his neck to his brown wool sweater.

A woman hurried past mustering a child in a pushchair and clutching around her head a flapping, broken umbrella. Josh's eyes followed her frantic scurry to a tenement block that hadn't seen a lick of paint since the 1960s. There was a splash and a sensation of freezing, mucky water seeping across the toes of his right foot. He had not seen the puddle straddling the pavement. Now his feet fair sang a squelching song.

By the time the shopping parade came into view the mizzle had stopped. The shops lined both sides of the road where cars were shoehorned bumper-to-bumper against the kerb, while the unlucky ones drifted up and down – vultures looking for a tasty parking space. It was a drab suburban scene of middle-aged housewives and pensioners jockeying for position amongst pound-a-time charity shops.

A scrap of a dog tied to a lamppost outside the bakery shop eyed Josh's squealching approach until he was within range then growled and leapt up. "Bugger aff!" Josh swiped his foot towards the dog then swerved from its sphere of influence. The detour took him within sniffing distance of the Charles Napier pub. And the rest, as Suzy would say, was history.

Three pints of heavy soon lightened the coinage in his pocket to 94 pence. Josh checked his pennies and scowled at the two greasy-haired skater punks seated near the door still cradling the same drinks they had been supping when he walked in. The wonky-toothed bartender returned. "Another?" he asked.

"Nah."

"Sticking on three, that's no you. Are you trying to get on the wagon?"

Josh reached across the counter and grabbed the bartender's waistcoat, almost ripping it.

"Trying to say I'm a lassie 'cause I've only had three?"

"Calm doon. I was jist saying I've no seen you aboot for a while," the bartender stuttered. Josh released his grip.

"I dinnae get the chance to come doon here often. No since that basketcase boss of yours barred me."

"Barred you?" the bartender's eyes popped. "Who did? Tommy? He's never said any'hing to me."

"Nah. No Tommy. Whit's his name. Old git with the boxed ears?"

"Campbell. He left years ago. I dinnae ken he'd barred you. Whit for?" The bartender took the dishtowel from off his shoulder and began polishing the wine glasses hanging from a rack the length of the bar, not that anyone ever ordered wine in Ferrybridge.

"Dancing," replied Josh.

"Dancing?"

"On the tables."

"Is that all. He barred you for that?"

"Well, that's whit I was doing before the rammy started, and it wisnae me who threw the first punch. One of them druggies from the estate kicked aff." Josh turned and looked hard at the yobs sitting near the door.

"Must have been my night aff." The bartender wiped another wine glass and tossed the towel back across his shoulder.

"Must have been." Josh turned to face him.

"So where are you drinking now?"

"The Gannet."

"The Gannet! That shit hole." The barman's wonky teeth hung out waiting for a slap. Josh restrained himself.

"Beer's all right."

"Must have changed then. Place was full of scumbags and toadies selling hot gear. That Stovey was a regular, always on the rob and dumping on anyone daft enough to buy aff him. Is he still doon there?"

Josh lifted his glass, downed the last dregs, and slammed it on the counter.

"Sure you'll no have another?" the bartender ventured.

Josh rattled the coins in his pocket. "Nah, I've got to keep the old woman happy."

"Aye, whatever."

Josh walked back outside onto the street where the mizzle was now remembered only in diminishing puddles. Over the heads of the milling shoppers he spied his quarry. The unsuspecting game was a few hundred metres down the road – rolls of carpet propped against the shop front, just waiting.

A thick, red carpet was furthest from the shop window. Josh fingered the price tag of forty-five pounds as it accidentally-on-purpose fell to the ground. Hidden from view of the shop window he crouched and grabbed the foot of the carpet, lifting it caber-fashion. Balancing against his right shoulder he started back along Ferrybridge Road, waddling under the weight. Approaching a trot he came past the Charles Napier pub again and veered sharp left down an alleyway into the back streets of an estate that led to the Bain housing scheme. No one opened their gob until he was in Easter Avenue where two identical ginger-haired boys, wearing tatty school uniforms, were kicking a football from kerb to kerb.

"Hey mister. What are you doing wi' that. Are you tossing the caber?" asked one of the 11-year-olds.

"Aye," Josh planted his feet firmly beneath him and hoisted the carpet upwards, launching it in a somersault through the air. It crashed onto the road ahead.

The twins laughed. "Rubbish. You'll no win at the 'ighland gemms wi that effort," the first joked.

"I'm no as good wi a carpet," Josh complained.

The second ginger-top rushed to the fallen slug of carpet and tried to lift its limp body. "Can I have a go?"

"Sure. Jist come and ask me when you're big enough to lift it."

Josh had not noticed the rapid approach of a shiny black mountain bike, it screeched to a sliding halt inches away. The lanky schoolboy riding the bike had a severe 'number one' all-over head shave. "What's going on?" he asked, stroking his convict haircut.

"We're practicing tossing the caber," answered the second twin, still struggling to lift the carpet higher than his waist.

"Wi a bit of carpet? Get a grip."

Josh bent and threw the carpet onto his right shoulder. It now resembled a warped red plank.

"Whose carpet is it anyhow?" the lanky boy pestered, almost running his front wheel over Josh's boots.

"Mine," said Josh.

"Bollocks is it. You're too fuckin' poor to have a carpet."

"Mind your fuckin' language or I'll gee you a swipe wi this." Josh twisted around, causing the carpet to sweep past the boy's head.

"Try it and I'll get ma faither on to you."

The ginger twins sat on the kerb watching, the football resting between them. "Leave him alone Gary," said one.

"So it's Gary is it?" Josh noted.

"Ma name's no important. Whit's important is you threatened me and ma dad'll whip you."

"Can he run fast?"

"Aye."

"Good, then I'll no need to gie him a heid start when I come round to sort him out." Josh resumed walking down the middle of the road. The boy followed on his bike. Nothing was said, but Josh wondered if the constant whirring noise behind him was the wheels of the bike or Gary's brain trying to think of a response. Then it came.

"You shouldn't make fun o' ma faither. Dae yi hear me?"

"Aye, but I wish to God I couldnae."

"Ma faither's in the polis. He'll arrest you, bang you up and throw away the key. So he will. Then you'll no think you're a big man."

Josh reached the crappy garden gate of home. "Why don't you shoo and play wi' your mates."

Convict haircut Gary pulled another over-dramatic skid. "I'm gaunae tell ma faither of you," he threatened.

"Oh aye, what are you going to tell him?"

"You nicked that carpet." He popped a wheelie and let the front wheel bounce back on the ground. "You've got nay money. You nicked that carpet and ma faither's going tae nick you."

"Bugger aff!" Josh bared his teeth.

Gary pulled back on his bike with a one-fingered salute. "Spin! I know where you live mister."

Josh fumbled with his key in the latch and swung open the front door. Suzy was halfway down the hallway, her disbelieving eyes bulging. Josh dropped the carpet.

"I'll lay it later. Have you got ma dole cheque?"

"In there," Suzy nodded towards the living room. The carpet transfixed her attention. Expecting it to be a figment of her imagination she prodded it, stroking the thick pile.

Josh re-emerged ready for action; a jacket in one hand, unemployment benefit cheque in the other. "See you later."

Satisfied with his philanthropy he was soon celebrating in The Gannet with Stovey and Angus bookending him at the bar. Angus was a giant of a man with arctic blond hair. He was still wearing his construction site clobber, caked in clay, mud and cement dust. He leaned his hefty frame against the bar for support as he moaned about criminally low wages.

"That's why you'll no find mugs like me and Josh slaving away for a living," Stovey piped up, with a satisfying smirk across his fake tanned face as he gripped his third pint of black and tan. Angus was a slow-moving hulk at the best of times and took an age to nod his head.

"You've got tae get your priorities sorted in this life. Jist look at Josh, he's got a carpet to lay at hame but he's in here socialising. That's what it's all aboot," Stovey continued. Josh nodded and took the last swig of heavy from his pint, raising his glass to alert Tom Tom, the barman, that a refill was needed pronto.

"It's a mug's game," Angus came back with a response to Stovey's last but one statement.

"Of course it is. Get some smarts big yin. Jafancy making a fortune like me on the free market or dae yi want keep slogging away building a toon centre library that nay fucker's going tae use?"

A fresh pint of heavy arrived, it's smooth body alive with carbonated action and a small head of white capping the brim like a slice of wild ocean. Josh savoured the texture as it slipped down his throat. The fifth pint of the night was always special, to be enjoyed with the least fuss. He avoided being dragged into the conversations flying around him. It wasn't until his pint was nearly empty, some twenty minutes later, that he heard Stovey address him.

"How did Suzy like the African man?" Stovey's lank hair flopped dangerously close to the top of his refreshed pint as he leaned sideways to catch Josh's attention.

"She didnae."

"What? No one could not like African man. That piece is worth hundreds. Did yi tell her?"

"I telt her, but she's got different ideas."

"Ach, that's a real shame. Still, I've got something you really can't do without."

Cold air rushed through the pub door as Stovey led the way to the rear car park. Josh clung to his pint, moving from the damp shadows into a circle of incandescent illumination panning down from an ancient light fitting high on the pub wall. Seven cars were parked. One was Stovey's faded blue Metro. All his wheeling and dealing had failed to elevate him in the automotive stakes, as testified by the rusting holes in the sills of his 20-year-old banger.

Even from the pub door it had been possible to see Stovey's latest 'bargain' – a six-foot diameter inverted pregnant belly satellite dish strapped to the Metro's roof.

"A full size satellite dish," Stovey stated the obvious.

"It's a bit big. I dinnae think it'll fit in the living room," Josh responded coolly.

"It's for ootside."

"Suzy wouldnae like it stuck on the wall."

"Nay problem. You mount it in the garden. It stands on its ain. And on this you can pick up any satellite station, and I mean any. There's a decoder box. Josh, this thing's magic. I've got one at hame and you should see the Swedish erotica."

Josh was sinking his pint of heavy at a steady rate of knots. He viewed the giant wok from all angles. "How much?"

"Normally I'd no let it go for less than a hundred, but you can have it for seventy."

Josh dropped his gaze and studied the gravel around Stovey's battered Doc Marten boots, then looked up. "I'll think about it." With that he walked back to the pub.

"Well, don't think too long 'cause I've a few others interested and they're prepared to pay full welly."

It was a welcome retreat to be back in the noisy huddle of drinkers where the fragrance of beer and fags clouded rational thought. Peter had arrived. The 64-year-old blind man was the most regular of regulars. He was dressed as usual in only underpants and vest and scuffed brown shoes, and leaned at his reserved spot at the far end of the bar, supping a black and tan.

"All right Peter?" Josh enquired as he passed. Peter raised his hand in acknowledgement and resumed his baggy-arsed slouch. He was the only drinker who could remember all seven past owners of The Gannet – and that carried major respect amongst the boozing fraternity. Josh aspired to such elevated status. He was already top dog in the drinking stakes, easily downing a dozen pints every night. He ordered his sixth bang on time – it is eight o'clock.

Big Angus turned to Josh and asked, "How do you keep your misses sweet?"

"How dae yi mean?"

"Coming here every night, drinking."

"I jist dae it. If she's got a problem wi it that's up to her. I dae what I want wi my money and she does her thing." Josh contemplated his refreshed pint, trying to think of a real answer.

"Mine'll no take it like that. She just says I piss my wages up the wall."

Josh laughed. "Well she's wrang. Hang on, I'm going to the bog."

"Aye, me too." Angus put his pint down and followed Josh to the toilets. "I try to tell her that it's my life and she just threatens to leave all the time, or smashes plates..." The two men entered the toilets and silence descended as they stood at the urinals, focusing on the pen-marked graffiti inches from their eyes. Josh was the first to leave. A moment later Big Angus followed, resuming his sentence where he had left off, "...all I want to do is have a few beers when I finish work. She cannae see it. She thinks I should be at home watching Eastenders wi her."

Josh nodded. "It's a shame. They don't get it. That's why there's nay women in the boozer. They don't understand the art of drinking. You can try and please them as much as you like but they'll never get it. And the more you try bending over backwards to please them the more they'll grind you doon until you're a lap dog or a rug for them to wipe their feet on." Josh reacquainted himself with his pint. "Take it from me, you've got to do your ain thing, and if she disnae like it she can sling her hook."

Angus rubbed his chin. "Bend over backwards to please them...how does that work?" Then, as he grabbed his pint, he laughed. "Och aye. I see. But all that work getting her in the first place. It's no right to throw away all that and then have to go through it all again to find another one."

"It's all priorities, and I dinnae worry aboot it," Josh downed the remainder of his pint and gestured for his seventh; Stovey sidled over to talk about the satellite dish.

CHAPTER FIVE

FACE TO FACE

Crispy bacon crackled in the frying pan, spitting a greasy aroma that interrupted Josh's drunken slumber. Eggs, toast, black pudding – he was picturing it all.

Opening his eyes there was only the living room ceiling. He was lying topless on the leather sofa. Daylight that was diffused through the curtains cast a pale gloss over the walls. He shifted on one elbow to stare at the bare floorboards and wondered about the carpet he'd snared the day before. Perhaps Suzy had stored it somewhere. He burped and rested on his back again.

"I'll have some breakfast," he called, not expecting a reply. He wasn't disappointed. The tormenting smell of breakfast cooking lasted for another ten minutes before the door swung open and Suzy carried a plate issuing steam.

"Is that fur me doll?" Josh ripped his skin from the leather sofa and sat to attention.

"In the name of…whit's that?" Suzy had seen it. To be fair it was hard to miss. The satellite dish sat upright, a six-foot bowl filling the floor. Through her heavier than usual mascara Suzy's eyes reddened.

"It's a dish for the telly, Hen. It goes in the garden," said Josh.

"No in oor garden it disnae."

"It'll be all right. Wait 'till you see the programmes you can watch."

"How much did you waste on it?"

Josh couldn't pry his eyes from the fried breakfast Suzy was holding just inches away. "No much, no much. It wis a bargain, less than fifty…"

"Fifty quid. You paid fifty quid for that?" Suzy's short peroxide hair shook as she tipped the breakfast into the middle of the gaping satellite dish. "There, you can eat oot of it, that's all it's good fur."

The bacon and black pudding slid to a small pile at the bottom of the dish. Josh groaned. "Ah Hen, that's no fair. I've been good to you this week. I got a carpet and I'll put it doon today."

"Carpet!" Suzy was on top form. "Dinnae carpet me!" She stormed out and returned with a scrap of paper that landed at Josh's bare feet. Josh could hardly focus, and his stomach was feeling queasy. "What's that?"

"A court summons."

"Whit?"

"The polis left it when they came last night and took the carpet back. The carpet you pinched." Suzy's shrouded black eyes burned through him, her arms were tightly crossed.

"Who did you show the carpet tae?"

"Nae one. They jist came and took it."

Josh punched a fist into his left hand. "That wee shite."

"You nicked it, didn't you."

"I was going to pay fur it."

"Pull the other one, it's got bells on. Josh, you're a waste of space. I didnae get involved wi you to waste ma life in a shit hole like this. I want more fae life. Mandy's got her own place and car. Tammy and Louise are going on a cruise. Murial's had a new kitchen…"

Josh raised his voice. "Is that what this is all aboot, keeping up appearances?"

"Keeping up appearances is something you'll never have to worry about," Suzy shouted back as she left, grabbing her coat from the hook beneath the hallway stairs.

Josh held his head in his hands as the front door slammed, pulling his feet upwards and lying back on the sofa. It was late into the afternoon before his hangover subsided enough for him to contemplate moving again. The fried breakfast had congealed in the centre of the satellite dish. The yellowing curtains were still drawn, but he knew Suzy was back. He had heard the door hours earlier and now there was the clatter of cutlery in the kitchen and the unmistakable, incomprehensible sound of her talking to herself. Josh didn't need to listen to know what the subject matter was. By the time he wheeled the satellite dish out through the patio doors into the back garden Suzy had materialised. The dish was propped against the wall, facing inwards.

"I'll fix it in the mourn'," Josh said, head down. Suzy did not respond, barely moving as he squeezed past to get back indoors. The arguments were bad but the silence that followed was ten times worse for Josh. By the time he'd cooked his fried lunch the kitchen was smoked out.

At four in the afternoon he walked out the front door, coat under arm, having not shared a word with Suzy. It was too early for The Gannet but he went anyway and found himself in the drinking company of strangers – afternoon regulars he never normally got to see. Tom Tom was serving.

"Early Josh," he observed, pulling a pint of heavy unbidden.

"Aye, nay reason to stay hame. I'm in the dog hoose again." Josh paid for his drink.

"Well, you're safe here."

Josh contemplated his bevvy. By eight o'clock he was on his tenth pint, well ahead of schedule. His co-ordination was going, his legs wobbled as he shifted his stance. Angus and Stovey were sober in comparison. Blind Peter arrived in his pants and vest and ordered his first. Josh piped up that he had to go. He made an ungraceful shift towards the door. Stovey was having none of it and blocked his exit.

"Go? What do you mean you have to go? You dinnae have to do anything, remember? You're the boss."

"I've got tae show responsibility," Josh slurred. "Suzy needs to see that I can go hame afore closing time."

Stovey grabbed Josh's arms as he wavered on the verge of falling. "You're no going anywhere. Drink, here Tom Tom, another pint o' heavy o'er here."

The pint was three-quarters empty when Josh seized his chance to slide away. Angus was having another bout of self doubt on the meaning of wife and Stovey was giving the keenest advice that only a freelance dick could. In the rarefied atmosphere of ale and fags it all made perfect sense, as did Josh's quiet getaway as he slunk from the bar. No one except the Y-fronted blind Peter noticed. "Bye Josh," he said without turning.

Car headlights flashed by outside. Josh was unaccustomed to so much activity on his wandering crawl home. Normally all he encountered were deserted streets, but having started his drinking session much sooner than usual he was now staggering home at a far earlier hour. The salt-riddled smell of the sea seasoned the night air as it occasionally did when the wind turned north across the Firth of Forth, refreshing the city and banishing the day's pollutants. The combination of warm, sea fragrant air and ten pints of heavy swung Josh from his path onto the main road where he boarded a claret-coloured double-decker bus to hasten his homeward journey. He fell asleep only to be woken by the driver shaking his right shoulder. "End of the line, pal," the driver said.

Josh rubbed his eyes, "Eh?"

"Time to get off. I'm going to the depot."

Josh peered out at the night. "Where's this?"

"Cramond," the driver replied, walking back to the front of the bus. He was a big man, more than a few stones overweight with hair cropped tight to his scalp.

"Eh? I didnae want to come here. I wis only going doon the road."

"If you wanted to get aff somewhere else you shouldn't have fallen asleep. Now come on, I've got a hame to go to," there was a hint of aggression in the driver's voice.

"So huv I. Take me back," Josh protested.

The driver wearily walked back and grabbed Josh's jacket lapels, pulling him from his seat. "Come on, off you get. I'm no messing aboot at this time o'night."

Josh was in no state to offer resistance. He managed a feeble two-fingered salute as the bus pulled off into the night. A nearby chip shop caught his attention and a few minutes later he emerged with a poke of chips reeking of salt and vinegar, which assaulted his senses as did the musty fragrance of seaweed as he zagzigged his way onto the dark expanse of Cramond Beach.

In the distance the lights of the Forth Road Bridge appeared as a blaze of faerie lanterns strung across the night, while slightly closer the cantilever majesty of its older sister, the Forth Bridge, was a dark silhouette. Reaching the last of the crispy chip ends Josh screwed up the paper wrapping and launched it with the tip of his boot into the darkness. "Worthy of Hampden Park," he congratulated himself.

The northern wind tugged his hair, pressing it backwards. Sea-salt tasted the air. The water's edge glistened in the distance beyond the grey sands lightly touched by a half-sulking moon.

What was the tide doing, stroking restlessly the bosom of the naked beach? Searching for something to steal? It grasped at stones and pebbles and carried them away to a secret horde beneath the water's inky depths. Straggly wisps of bobbled seaweed reached for the safety of land but were only a tide away from being gobbled once more by the greedy master whispering at their tails.

Into this dark theatre Josh slumped, his arse unceremoniously hitting dry sand. Resting arms on knees he devoured the splendor of moonlight dancing across the ever-forming waves that rippled all the way to Fife on the opposite shore. From here it was possible to see more than ten miles away to the dark hills and mountains of the north, and the pinpricks of distant streetlights across the water. He had never crossed to Fife and now he wondered how different it would be. Perhaps there was someone over there sitting on the sand right now reflecting on the lights of Edinburgh, pondering the same thoughts.

A lone seagull, a phantom against the night, cried as it ghosted past. It took Josh back to his childhood and endless days of adventure brimming with friends, exploring rock pools and seashores. Where were those pals now? Where had life taken them that they were never to be seen around the streets of the housing scheme? Some were married, some had kids, others had taken to the road and discovered careers and well-paid jobs away from the city, away from Scotland, Katrina amongst them. They had gone. But their playful cries lived on here where the River Forth – more sea than fresh water – scoured the sands daily carrying memories of days past.

And where was Josh? Nowhere. He was a dropout unable to work; a drinker and a waster. He grabbed some sand. Anger tightened his hand into a fist, and he crushed the sand into a ball and launched it before him. The breeze exploded the ball sending gritty granules back into his face. "Thanks," he spluttered, clearing his lips and rubbing his eyes. "I know I shouldnae drink but I cannae help it. There's nowt else for me, can you no see that?"

Only the river that thought it was a sea listened.

"I've been a waster too long to change. If I was going to be anything else it would have happened by now. I'm 36 and there's no way back for me. I try to cut the swallying but it's nae good. It's all I've got left."

Carried on the northern breeze a distant whistling barely existed but was there all the same. Was it the wind blowing through the girders of the rail bridge he mused? His eyes were once more drawn to where the great Victorian era edifice floating high above the moon-danced water. The sound became clearer, defining into a song of lilting beauty seducing his mind. He lay back and gazed at wandering clouds, their edges silver-gilted by the moon's glow, sliding silently across the starry mosaic. His world was spinning. The whistling lament a psychedelic soundtrack accompanying the kaleidoscopic starry night. Then there was a voice, as faint and airy as the wind through the cables of the far off suspension road bridge and the steel lattices of the rail bridge.

"What's the swallying?" the voice asked.

Josh swung his head left and right as he searched for the speaker. Twisting around he found only the dark cloak of night.

"So?" the voice teased. This time Josh leapt to his feet, standing tall against the tricks of the unknown. A cloud flitted across the moon, dimming the nocturnal illumination that coated a large rock five steps to his right. Almost as quickly the cloud cleared away, and as the moonlight stroked the beach once more he saw something unnaturally white barely visible beside the rock. It was a woman with the milky white skin and flowing blonde hair of a sun-bleached Greek statue.

"Do I know you?" he asked.

"Should you?" she replied.

"What?" Josh wondered if he should approach her. "Are you a bampot?"

The woman remained frozen, half hidden behind the rock. "Are you scared of me?"

"No. Just a little surprised that someone else is down here at this time of night." It was the fastest he had ever sobered up. He needed his wits, this could be a trap, she might have accomplices sneaking up. He checked over his right shoulder, but there was no one.

"Can I borrow your coat?" she asked quietly.

"What?"

"Your coat. I haven't anything to wear."

Damn, now Josh knew he was drunk. He slapped his right hand hard against his forehead and stared down at his feet, whispering as he counted to ten. When he looked up the young woman in her 20s was still there peeking at him from behind the rock, the wind blowing her long, golden hair until it caught on her lips like wisps of smoke streaking across her face.

"Where are your clothes?" Josh asked.

"I haven't any."

"You walked down here in the noddy?"

"No."

"No?"

"I swam," she replied.

Josh tried to comprehend for a moment, his head involuntarily shaking slightly from side to side then he started undoing the buttons on his leather jacket. He walked a few steps towards the rock and tossed the jacket far enough that the woman was able to catch it without revealing herself. She vanished from sight with the jacket. Josh waited.

A few minutes passed.

"Are you still there?" Josh dragged a hand though his hair and waited some more. "Shite! I knew this was gonna happen." He strode forward expecting to find the woman and his jacket gone, but there she stood, bare-legged and shoe-less, wearing his jacket that reached to her knees.

"I can't do it up," she said, fumbling with the buttons. Josh approached and forced them through the holes. He could smell the sea on her skin and in her hair.

"Where do you live?" he asked. She did not reply, but looked deeply into his eyes then out over his left shoulder to the black expanse of the Forth estuary.

"Oot there? You've swum all the way from Fife, jeez," Josh was momentarily mesmerised by the delicate paleness of her blue eyes. "Well, there's no way you're going to get back tonight, daftie. Here, I'll put you up fur the night. You can borrow some of Suzy's clothes."

"Are you sure?"

"Nae problem. You stay oot here all night you'll catch your death." Josh led her from the beach. She followed, one step behind. Her bare feet glided over the sand, but once on the stone path she started to hobble as the sharp ground bruised her soles. Her arms were wrapped tightly around the jacket.

Half-a-mile on, having barely spoken, they reached the bus stop. On the opposite side of the road was the fish and chips shop where Josh had earlier bought his supper. A car drove by and a skin-headed youth in the passenger seat leaned out and wolf whistled at the blonde woman's bare legs. "Wrong area, love," he called.

"Fuck off," Josh gave a one-fingered salute. As they stood at the bus shelter there were more car horn blasts, but they could not mask the silence between the woman and Josh. Feeling increasingly uncomfortable Josh offered his name and asked the woman hers. She shook her head.

"You ain't got a name?"

Her blonde locks swayed as she stared out across the road. "Pukka," she said.

"Pukka? What sort of name is that?" Josh followed her eyes and saw the illuminated Pukka Pies sign over the fish and chips shop.

"Pukka. Pukka Pies. Come of it, that's not your name. What's wrong, are you running away from someone, is that it?"

"Will you hold me, please," the woman asked, keeling forward. Josh caught her shivering body, putting an arm around her waist as support. As he did so the late night bus pulled up at the stop. The driver gave a knowing smile as Josh paid for two tickets.

"It's not what you think," was all Josh could think to say as he led the woman to the back seat, under scrutiny from two teenagers and an old man who sat near the middle of the bus. Josh watched the woman closely as she rested on the seat. The effort of her night swim had sapped her strength, she could barely keep her eyes open, and her unnaturally white skin was icy cold to the touch.

The bus journey took half an hour. There were no lights on when Josh arrived home, earlier than usual but much later than he had planned. Suzy had gone to bed.

"You'll be all right once you're warmed up. I'll get the fire on," he reassured the woman as they neared the front door. As he practically carried her weakening body towards the house he did not notice an upstairs curtain twitch. Suzy watched the pair's progress from the bedroom window. She listened to the latchkey quietly opening the front door. Without switching a light she moved to the top of the stairs, watching from the darkness as the strange woman, who appeared paralytic and unable to co-ordinate her movements, was carried inside. Only when Josh had taken the woman out of sight into the living room did Suzy return to her bed, burying herself beneath the blankets. The house was still again, the only noise Suzy's muffled sobs.

CHAPTER SIX

SUZY'S DECISION

Suzy watched as the first light of the morning slid a finger along the curtain edges. She was normally the first to rise in the house but today she lay late beneath the lemon quilt, staring at the pattern of summer flowers on the curtains. She listened to the metronome snoring of Josh downstairs. He had never brought a woman home before. In all his drunken stupors he had never had the gall to do that. Now he had, and worse he had come home early – before pub throwing-out time. What was he trying to prove?

She slowly pushed back the quilt and reached for clothes in the wardrobe. She felt passive and unwanted. There was no thought in the colours she chose. The red skirt and yellow blouse had never matched before but today they would do. Her white slippers had not been worn since Christmas week, but now they were fished from the bottom of the wardrobe. Pulling open the curtain she observed another non-descript grey day brooding over the tenements. Then she stood at the landing at the top of the stairs. Josh's snoring was louder. A draft twitched at the wind chime by the front door as it always did. She listened for any other noise but there was none, not even a whisper from the hussy, but she knew she was down there wrapped beside Josh or sprawled discarded across the floor.

For a long moment she listened to the silence of the house and children playing in the street on the way to school. Then she slowly began to descend the stairs.

Josh was blissfully unaware of any of this. Asleep on the sofa, his alcohol-addled mind was entangled in dream.

He was wandering down a long corridor of his old school, trying each of the classroom doors in turn but finding them all locked. There was no one around. In the cloakroom he bent over a drinking fountain, but it is dry. There was not a single drip no matter how hard he pushed at the cold chrome knob. He licked his cracked lips, his parched throat cried out for some relief.

Between the pegs of the cavernous cloakroom hung a few forgotten blazers and an old, mud-encrusted, red rugby shirt. Staring through the dangling items, he caught sight of movement at the far end of the room. It was a dark-haired girl. As he called out to her she darted away through the swinging doors. He gave chase, his feet skidding as he turned around the tight corners of the rows of cloakroom pegs and burst through the double doors that led back into the school corridor. There was no one there, but a door leading outside to the playground rocked gently.

A blooming cherry tree was a riot of colour, swaying in the breeze where it stood on a grass island beside the school gates. A few red and white petals were gently falling on the grass. Beyond the tree the dull brown of the bicycle shed hid dark shadows, but there was no one there. The school grounds appeared deserted. Josh listened to his own heavy breathing. He then turned to his right and walked past a dumped pile of coal coke next to the school kitchen. The dirty fuel was waiting for someone to shovel it into a basement bunker to feed the boilers below. Still there was no sign of the dark-haired girl.

Around another corner, cocooned in its private hanger, an indoor swimming pool was visible through a set of floor-to-ceiling windows. The pool water was flat and undisturbed. Continuing on, Josh was soon at the edge of the school's main playing field. It was devoid of any signs of life, its vastness enhanced by its emptiness. The grassy field stretched away, coming to an end against the brick walls of terraced gardens on the far side. On the school side of the field was a short row of 100-year-old elm trees. Josh wondered about the people who had planted them and what they would have thought now if they could see how the elms had grown to tower over the tired classrooms.

Almost blending in with one of the tree trunks was the dark-haired girl. She took flight again the moment his eyes picked her out. She was heading for the front of the school, but Josh wouldn't lose her for a second time. He sprinted hard towards the trees and called her name "Katrina!" but the harder he tried to run the more he seemed to go nowhere and his feet slipped in the greasy mud beneath the trees. He called the girl's name again, and even as he did there was another voice calling out from behind him. It was calling his name louder and louder.

"What?" he answered, and as he did he stumbled in the mud, his foot sticking fast as he pitched forward and pushed his arms out to break his fall.

"Where is she?" the voice behind him shouted.

"Roond the corner," Josh answered, feeling himself hitting the muddy ground even as he kept his eyes focused on the corner of the school building where the girl had vanished.

His body jerked as he teetered on the edge of the sofa. Suzy shoved him back to stop him falling off.

"Roond the corner is she?" Suzy slapped him a smart one. She looked around the room and, seeing no one, dished another ringing slap to Josh's face. "Wake up, where is she?"

Josh's eyes were open but he could see only fuzziness, his cheeks stung and he held his hands up to protect against further blows, trying at the same time to rub the sands of sleep away. "What's up?"

"Where is she?" Suzy repeated, towering above the sofa, hands thrust against her red-skirted hips.

"Who?" Josh tried to pull himself up, but his left arm had been trapped beneath his sleeping body and denied a proper blood flow. It was now a useless dead weight.

"That hussy you brought back fae the pub last night."

Josh scratched his head and looked around. His jacket wasn't lying in the middle of the floor – that was unusual. Sitting up proved to be a bad move, his head spun. As his left foot rotated off the sofa it sent a nearly empty bottle of Johnnie Walker Red Label whisky clattering onto the wooden floorboards. Suzy kicked the bottle with one of her white-slippered feet.

"I've had enough of this Josh. I'm sick to the back teeth of having to put up with you pissing oor money up the wall every night, bringing crap into the hoose and insulting me with...," but she could not finish the sentence. Tears overtook her. She looked away. Josh searched for something to say. The house was silent except for Suzy's half-stifled sobs. Then there was another sound, a splash of water from the bathroom upstairs. Suzy froze, then she turned to stare at Josh sprawled uselessly on the sofa. There was another splash. It was unmistakable.

"She's up there," Suzy concluded, then much louder, "She's up there, isn't she?"

Josh could not find words quickly enough to respond before Suzy vanished in a whirling blur of yellow and red, her slippered feet angrily thumping up the stairs. Reaching the bathroom door she pushed it wide open. Daylight caught something shiny in the bath. Josh's leather jacket floated in the tub. A few strands of long blonde hair were stuck against its collar. Then the jacket moved. There was a squeak and a long, sleek snout rose up from beneath.

"In the name of!" Suzy's voice trailed into nothing as her right hand reached across her mouth.

≈

Josh was where Suzy had left him, half asleep and fully hungover, sprawled on his back on the sofa with his left leg hanging over the edge. The Johnnie Walker bottle was lying in the middle of the floor where she'd kicked it. Suzy dropped her suitcase hard onto the floor beside her, causing the slumbering, steaming Josh to awaken with a start.

"What….what's happening love?" Josh brushed a hand across his eyes as he focused on Suzy, who now wore a brown jacket that almost reached to the bottom of her red skirt. Her white slippers had gone, replaced by brown knee-length boots.

"I'm off. You can get your lady friend to cook and wash for you."

"Suzy, I cannae remember last night. She must have followed me hame. I didnae pick her up, that's no me, you know that's no me."

"You're still drunk. Wait 'til you've sobered up and then take a good, long look at what you've done." Suzy lifted her suitcase and turned on heels of her boots. "Got any excuse for the dolphin?" she threw out as she marched from the room.

"Whit?" Josh half-tumbled from the sofa onto his feet and staggered to follow her. The front door was already open as he entered the hallway. Suzy looked back with a face of thundering defiance.

"The dolphin in the bath. You see, you can't even remember that. You're a waster, that's what you are." Suzy turned and headed out of the door. Josh tried to move to stop her but stumbled and fell, cracking his head on the stair banister. Blood immediately streaked across his temple as he pushed himself back up from the floor.

"Suzy, dinae go. I'll make it up." His calling was forlorn and in vain. He slumped against the door which banged shut with the weight of his crumpled body pressing against it. The blood from the cut above his right eye dripped onto his jeans. He no longer had the inclination to co-ordinate his arms or his legs.

Seven hours later the last of the day's grey light cast a morbid pall that hung like smoke in the air of the dingy hallway. Josh stirred to life, pain jabbed his back in protest at the hours it had been curled awkwardly against the front door. The wound to his temple was now a bloody, congealed hard lump. He stood up, unsure, wobbling and half-falling into the living room as he used the wall as a sliding support. The empty whisky bottle still lay abandoned on the floor. A nauseous feeling came over him again and the urge to reach the bathroom obliterated all other thoughts. He lumbered back into the hallway. As he ascended the stairs each upwards stumbling step pitched him either against the wall or stair banister for support.

Barging through the bathroom door, his mission almost complete, he saw the toilet pan. His stomach churned uncontrollably, but before he sank to his knees his eyes swivelled to the bathtub - and a dolphin staring up at him. Everything stopped, even the queasy sick gurgling within the back of his throat. Throwing himself backwards, he grabbed the door handle and pulled the door closed, half to shut out the image of the creature in the bath, half to prevent himself from falling backwards.

His stomach juices burst back into activity, building in power from deep within, sending his abdominal muscles into a spasm as he fought to stop the bile erupting. Ricocheting off the wall and bending the banister with his weight, he half fell down the twelve stairs. Just managing to stay upright he swung around off the bottom step and was carried by an unlikely providence to the kitchen sink where he threw up. The sour taste of whisky scorched the inside of his mouth, poisoning his taste buds as it was ejected. Water streamed from eye ducts and splashed down as his body quivered in pity and he hung, spent, on the stainless steel rim of the sink, wanting only to fall to the ground like a wounded animal.

It was dark when he was next aware of his surroundings. The linoleum of the kitchen clung to his sweaty body. He peeled himself off the floor and stared down the hallway at the front door where a hazy, iridescent orange streetlight was visible through the opaque glass. His head felt just as hazy as it spun with a disjointed stream of nightmare images.

"Suzy?" He called to the silence of the house. She was gone. That was not part of any imaginary nightmare. She was gone, he was drunk and had done something so stupid that she had packed her suitcase and stormed out. He lifted his right hand and slapped it against his forehead, but it failed to jolt his memory. His brain felt like it was floating in an alcohol rich sea of liquid sloshing around inside his head.

"What did I do?" He formed the words and listened as they echoed around the empty kitchen and hall. In the gloom of the unlit house he walked towards the front door and saw the glistening evidence of puke and blood. He groaned as he reached the living room, his fingers flapping like the wings of a lost bat as he searched for the light switch and then wished he hadn't as a dazzling brightness temporarily blinded him before subsiding enough to allow his eyes to alight on Johnnie Walker, all jolly hat and walking stick like a man who'd never tasted the guilty thump of a hangover. There were worse discoveries to come as he scanned the room. The corner cabinet beyond the dinner table and its towering bar stools was open, the door far enough ajar to reveal the bottles of spirits stored inside had been disturbed. The Johnnie Walker Red Label was already accounted for, lying as it did in the middle of the floor, but within the cabinet was its brother Johnnie Walker Black Label lying on his side, empty, and next to that the useless vessel of a full size Absolut Vodka bottle.

Josh took it all in. No wonder the demons have kidnapped his mind and senses all day and into the bleak evening. He had no recollection of partaking in a house-bound drinking spree the previous evening. A huge gapping hole of time and space had cut him adrift from his last known moment of competent thought when he had left The Gannet and jumped on a bus to Cramond Beach.

He removed the two empty bottles from the corner cabinet and closed the door with his left foot. He gathered up the Red Label from the floor. The bottles clinked together as he carried them to the kitchen and out through the back door to the garden. There was a crash as he dropped them in the plastic green wheelie bin parked against the fence. Propped between the fence and the house, like an oversized bathtub, was the satellite dish.

Images of Cramond Beach sprang into his mind like courtroom accusations. The drunken veils began to lift and he pictured again the silhouette of the Forth Bridge that had so transfixed him the previous evening, and the swift traverse of clouds through the moon-illuminated night sky. And then there was the woman. Yes, the naked woman with the golden hair.

He closed the back door and secured it with the key that always remained in the lock. He hurried back through the kitchen into the hallway, his dimmed senses now picking up the unmistakable fragrance of salty seawater. It wasn't a dream. Things were starting to fall into place....yes, he walked the woman to the bus stop and then he had brought her back to the house. That's what Suzy had been saying. She must have seen him. For a moment he hesitated at the foot of the stairs, staring up into the darkness of the unlit house as night wrapped around every corner. His right hand slapped against his forehead again as he swore to himself.

'So where is she now?' he asked. Maybe she had crept away in the night, disgusted after he'd drunk the whisky and vodka. Perhaps she had helped him drink it. No...now he was being stupid. The poisoning of his body was great enough to account for all the missing alcohol.

Scattered memories of the past twenty-four hours churned and swirled. His head dropped as he gripped the banister at the foot of the stairs, distracted by another thought. He stumbled to the living room, dazzled again by the light from the bare bulb hanging in the centre of the room. There was a scrap of paper on the sofa. Grabbing it, he read the police summons requesting his attendance to explain how he had come into the possession of a roll of carpet belonging to Richard's Carpets Limited.

He groaned. No one had followed him back from Ferrybridge, he had made sure of that by ducking through the alleys and taking the long route through the estate to lose any followers. The only ones who'd seen him had been the street kids. That's who it had been, that loud mouth kid must have grassed him up to his copper father.

"Bastard!" he swore, throwing the summons back onto the sofa. He swore again, this time louder as he remembered the bathroom and the dolphin that had stared at him from the bathtub.

"Shit!" Dumb things were his stock in trade of late, but this took the biscuit. He'd been drunk when he'd gone to the bathroom earlier, he told himself. It must have been a hallucination. There was no way he had carried a dolphin into the house.

Once more at the foot of the stairs, he stared into the now impenetrable dark above and began to climb, one cautious step at a time. The only light cutting through the nocturnal shadows came from the few shafts escaping from the open door of the living room below. In the semi-darkness he winced with each creaking stair. The bathroom door was closed. The door was never closed unless someone is inside.

"I closed it," he reassured himself, before halting at the top of the stairs, inches from the door.

"Hello," he said, ignoring his own weak reassurance from moments before. "Is there anyone up here?" There was no response. He reached forward. The knuckles of his right hand tapped against the door.

"Hello," a female voice responded.

Startled, Josh jumped back, his heart failed to register a couple of beats as the door slowly opened from within. In the darkness the blonde-haired woman he had met on the beach stood holding a purple towel tightly around her body. Water dripped from her hair and feet. Even in the darkness her blue eyes shone, captivating Josh, pulling him in. He did not see his own reflection in her eyes, instead there was Cramond Beach. And there he was, a youngster with a dark-haired girl companion called Katrina. Transfixed, he stared deeper into the woman's eyes and watched an unfolding re-run of the day, more than 20 years before, when he and Katrina had saved the baby dolphin. Everything was so clear, as though it had all just happened. Then the images faded and he was once more staring at the woman swaddled in the bathroom towel.

"That was you?" he asked.

She nodded.

"You're trying to tell me you were the dolphin?" He shook his head even as the words come out, surely the heavy drinking session of the previous night had worn off by now.

"You saved my life then, when I was young. You took the boys away from me and let me return to the water to recover as the tide took me back to deeper waters where my family waited."

The gloom of night had all but swallowed up the woman's shape and Josh was once more aware of the lack of light in the house, only the faintest glow from the downstairs living room doorway reached them. He stretched out and flicked the stair landing light, as he did the woman blinked as she adjusted to the sudden brightness.

"I'm no understanding, hen. How are you a woman if you're saying you're a dolphin?" Josh asked.

"There are no impossibilities," she replied, wrapping the towel tighter against her body.

"Come again?" Josh quizzed, almost sarcastically, as he began to sense he was the fall guy for some elaborate joke. But he could detect no hint of play-acting from the woman, even though he now watched her every facial movement like a hawk.

"You see me as I want you to see me, but I can not hold this form very long. Are you willing to help me again?"

"Help you? What do you want fae me?" Josh scratched his head, still unsure if he was dreaming.

"Return me to my family, my group out in the sea river," her head gestured to her left, as if sensing the direction of some ghostly saltwater impregnated breeze. "I have only a few days to rejoin them before they must leave for the summer seas in the north. If they leave without me I have little chance of making it on my own."

Josh shook his head. "Sorry hen, but this is too weird. I'm no buying that you're a dolphin."

"Did you not see me earlier, when I was in the bath?"

"I was drunk," Josh replied.

"Not so much that you didn't see me." She took the smallest of steps towards him.

"If you're what you say you are, then why did you leave the water? Why didn't you stay in the sea?"

The woman bowed her head. Her long, damp hair tumbled across her face as she looked down to her bare feet. One arm gripped the towel tightly around her slim body, the other reached up sweeping her hair back from her face as she looked at him again.

"I caught a virus, something in the water that wasn't good, a chemical. It turned me blind, shut off my ability to find my way until I ended up going around in circles as the water became shallower and shallower until I was stranded on the beach as the tide receded, unable to catch my breath." She stopped for a moment as she remembered.

"I was stranded once before, when I was young, but as you know I survived then because I was put back into the water. This time that was not the case and I was weak and hungry. My only chance was to find help."

Josh took in the words, as muddled as they were. "If you can change into a woman surely you could have walked back to the water and changed back into a dolphin, if that's the truth."

The woman shook her head. "No, I would merely have thrown myself back into danger, still affected and unable to feed or fend for myself, unable to find my family group. Rocks could smash my body, nets could haul me from the water and then it would all be over." She fell silent and stared downwards. Her legs began to buckle at the knees.

"Are you okay?" Josh stepped forward to offer support, his hand touching her right forearm. Her skin was much cooler than he expected.

She looked up again. "I have very little strength in this form. I need to rest."

Josh placed his left arm around her waist and led her to the master bedroom. The bed was neatly made, as Suzy had left it before she walked out. The room hung heavy with Suzy's musk perfume. In the darkness that was brightened only slightly by the streetlights outside, he let the woman sit on the edge of the bed, while he found the light switch. As the room lit up Josh turned to find the woman had already rested across the bed, curled up and apparently falling asleep with the damp towel her blanket. As she lay resting her breathing was as soft as a summer breeze twisting smoothly through a seashell. He wrapped the bed's lemon quilt around her and sat on the dressing chair in the corner, observing the gentle rise and fall of her body as she breathed.

She slept through the night but awoke in distress. Josh was shaken from his sleep, his body stiffened from the seated position he had kept all night. "What's wrong?" he asked as he rubbed his bleary eyes.

"I can't keep this form any longer, I need to get into water again." Even as the words hung in the air the woman was heading out of the room, the towel still held against her as she returned to the bathroom. There was an explosion of noise as the cold water tap was turned on full blast.

"Salt, I need salt in the water. Please," she called back.

Josh stood up, stretching his aching back. "What kind of salt?"

"Any, just dissolve it in the water. Please hurry."

Down the stairs Josh trotted, this time more in control of his body, finally free from his hangover. He noticed the living room light had been left on all night. In the kitchen he hunted for salt. There was a small shaker in the condiments cupboard next to an upside down ketchup bottle. Beyond, and partially hidden behind a large vinegar bottle, was a plastic container with a drawing of a whale breaching on its side.

"Sea salt, perfect," he congratulated himself and pulled it out, knocking over the ketchup in the process. As he turned he caught sight of movement outside the window in the back garden. It was still early morning, but not so early that the local schoolboys weren't out and about. He recognised the trio in the garden, it was the ginger-haired twins and the convict haircut boy from the day before. The three were guising around, climbing on the storm-damaged wooden fence that formed a now ineffective barrier between the garden and the allotments.

"Bugger aff!" Josh shouted, opening the back door. The three boys jumped down and vanished from sight.

The tap that had been pummeling water into the bathtub was silent by the time Josh once more ascended the stairs to the bathroom. Entering the room he saw the purple towel lying on the floor. The woman was gone. An adult dolphin lay in the overflowing bath, its right eye looking up at him.

"Shite, how am I gonna tell how much salt to put in now?" He opened the top of the sea salt container and began sprinkling the contents into the bathtub, swirling the water as he did so. "Is that enough?" There was no reply from the dolphin. He poured more. The container was almost half empty when the dolphin let out a high-pitched squeak.

"That's enough is it?" He stopped pouring, wiping sweat from his forehead. Then he heard a voice.

"Ah, I'm telling ma da'. You've got a dolphin in your bath!"

Josh looked up at the open bathroom window to see the face of the short-haired boy squeezing through the gap, eyes bulging as he looked at the dolphin. "Get off the fucking satellite dish!" Josh yelled back.

CHAPTER SEVEN

FORTH BRIDGE

Katrina lowered her eyes and contemplated the choppy waves a hundred feet below in the river that thought it was a sea. Even at such a distance the cold water reached up with invisible hands chilling her face. She looked away and up towards the soaring magnificence of the Forth Bridge, a marvel of the Victorian age. Its rugged splendor matched the wilderness it adorned. It belonged and it was hard to imagine a time before, or to come, when the railway bridge would not stand sentinel over the Forth's murky waters.

Standing inside the belly of the three-humped red monster she was a lost ant buffeted by the incessant wind whistling and swirling through this steel behemoth.

On many occasions as a schoolgirl she had looked across from Cramond Beach at the bridge never thinking that one day, more than 20 years later, she would walk along its high, treacherous platforms.

She glanced back to the shore where her car was now a dot in an empty car park. In the wind her scattered black hair danced on her shoulders as she squinted to see a group of men painting the steel latticework on a platform above.

"Anything I can help you with, lady?" asked a sepulchral voice. Katrina's heart skipped a beat. With a face beaten by a thousand storms, a tall and aged workman stood beside her rubbing greasy gunk between his fingers.

"Oh, yeah. When…what happens when you've finished painting the bridge. Do you go back to the start?" she asked. The silver-haired workman's eyes twinkled as he laughed, but his voice remained as hollow as the steel pipe-work.

"Aye, job's so big it's never done."

Katrina nodded and swept her eyes along the length of the bridge. "And how many people have you got?"

"Ten – when they're all here, mind."

"You're the boss?"

"Foreman. And no one else is supposed to be up here, you ken." The workman's tone changed as he wondered if this smartly dressed young woman before him was from health and safety, or worse.

"I was looking for someone. I thought they might be doing this job."

"What's their name?"

"Josh…Josh Robertson."

The foreman thought for a moment. "Nah, sorry. There's no one here with that name. Are you sure they said they were working on this bridge?"

Katrina forced a smile. "No. I wasn't sure. And I've not seen them for a long time. Sorry to trouble you." She turned and started to walk back the way she had come.

The foreman called out after her. "Nay trouble. Hope you find him." But his words were lost to the wind.

Katrina could see her car in the distance; it took another fifteen minutes to reach it. The northerly wind had increased in strength and was much colder. She hurried to close the door behind her and sat for a moment staring through the windscreen at the dimly lit outline of the Forth Bridge spanning the dark waters of the firth. A blinking red light near her feet caught her attention. It was her mobile phone. She had not noticed it fall from her coat pocket earlier. She retrieved it. There was one missed call and one voice message, but the display informed her the battery was exhausted. The message would have to wait.

CHAPTER EIGHT

FLATMATES

Katrina flung her hair backwards with a swift head jerk as she pulled the plug from the depths of the sink's soapsuds. Last night's dishes sparkled on the draining board, as did her breakfast bowl. She dried her hands on a towel by the window and looked out at the broken clouds galloping across the Edinburgh rooftops. Straightening her white blouse inside her dark skirt she walked into the living room, checking her face in the mirror as she passed and glancing at the video recorder's emotionless clock. It was eight-thirty.

"Lisa, are you up yet?" her voice bounced through the two-bedroom flat. "It's nearly nine."

"It's what?" a frantic, distant voice replied.

There was a crash and the sound of bare feet slapping across the floor. Lisa burst into the kitchen, her head an explosion of brown hair. Pink elephants were marching across her pyjamas trunk-to-tail. She spotted the clock on the wall. "Half eight! What are you trying to do to me?"

"Trying to get you to work on time for a change." Katrina brushed her hair so it curled upwards off her shoulders.

"I'll make it."

Katrina's disbelieving eyes doubted.

"I will. I'll make it up in flexi-time. I prefer working late anyway." Lisa reached for a slice of toast on Katrina's abandoned plate. "Do you want this?"

Katrina shook her head and watched Lisa bite into the lukewarm slice.

"What time did you get in last night, I didn't hear you?" Katrina asked.

"No idea, late. How was your night?"

"Crap. I've had it with bars, nothing but drunken jerks that can't keep their hands to themselves. This town is full of them and they're all the same."

"Gee, that bad huh?"

Katrina wandered back into the living room. "Have you seen my cap?"

Lisa followed and saw Purshaw preening herself in her new cat basket – Katrina's upturned cap. She waved her half-eaten slice of toast at the black cat and mouthed the word "shoo" under her breath. Purshaw ignored her. Katrina noticed Lisa's unsuccessful efforts. "Purshaw, out!" she shouted and the cat instantly bounded away as Katrina collected her cap, straightened the Scottish Society for the Protection of Animals badge on the front and brushed out a few cat hairs.

"Sorry," Lisa offered, scowling at Purshaw. "Hey, did you go down to the bridge yesterday?"

"Yes, after I'd given up on the bars."

"And? Was he there?"

"No. They'd never heard of him." Katrina straightened her cap in the mirror. "It was always a long shot."

"So what now? Have you tried the phone book?"

Katrina rolled her eyes towards the ceiling. "Do you know how many Robertsons are listed?"

"I'll give you a hand. We can do a couple each night," Lisa offered, finishing the toast and licking her fingers.

"Thanks. But maybe he's moved away. You know, it's twenty years ago, more even. He's probably married."

Lisa wrapped an arm around her flatmate. "Come on, be positive."

"I'm being realistic." Katrina grabbed her jacket and headed for the door.

"Look, we'll get the phone book out tonight and give it a shot, eh?" Lisa called.

Katrina stopped and turned. "Phone, thanks for reminding." She went back to the kitchen where her mobile phone was on the counter by the toaster where she had left it charging overnight. A blinking red light indicated a missed call; she listened to the message.

Lisa watched her friend's facial expression. "Something interesting?"

Katrina shook her head. "Someone's got a dolphin in their house. Oh joy, it's got to be wind-up. Just what I need to start the day."

She lowered the phone from her ear and tapped in a number. "Hello, Alec. Yeah, just got your message. Where is it? Oh, there. I might have guessed. Okay, I'm heading in now."

She put the phone into her jacket pocket, sighed and looked at Lisa. "Are you sure we can't swap jobs?"

Lisa smiled and watched her flatmate head out the door.

CHAPTER NINE

A REUNITING

"Fucking hell, what time do you call this? Your Suzy been cracking the whip or summit?" Stovey was ever ready with the welcome, blowing his eyes as large as they could go into saucer-shaped orbs of mocking surprise and milking his hard-drinking credentials. Truth was, in the drinking stakes, Josh could see him under the table on any given day of the week. The words 'light' and 'weight' always sprang to mind, and to tongue, when he was arguing with Stovey over who was the drinking king. But now Stovey seized his chance to be lord of the bar, even if it was only for one night. He swayed dangerously holding his pint.

"This is ma' tenth man. And where has youse been? Doing the washing up for the misses?" Stovey was enjoying giving a good rubbing and he was finding a ready audience judging by the ripple of laughter from the corner of the bar.

"Dinnae push it Stove. I'll drink twelve before you've finished your next." Josh had no intention of fulfilling his idle threat, but Stovey grabbed the bait like a kamikaze trout and downed his remaining half pint, banging the glass on the counter with a burp of satisfaction.

"You're on," Stovey announced. Josh got eight pints into the challenge before Stovey next banged his empty glass on the counter in triumph. "So you were saying," he smirked.

Josh felt his bloated stomach turning itself over as he tried to cope with the sudden influx of alcohol. At least now he could slow down, albeit with the damage done and the harping voice of Stovey haunting for the remainder of the night. In his rapidly growing state of inebriation, the words he expelled next were not what he intended, nor was the volume under his control.

"So who kens anything aboot making dolphins better?"

Stovey's gob fell out of action for a moment, unable to configure a reply to anything that did not involve alcohol and large quantities. He contented himself with a volley of burps.

"What do you want to know aboot that fur?" Big Angus had been holding his own counsel most of the night, but now involved himself in the group dynamic with Josh present. Tom Tom stood at the back of the counter listening. Blind Peter, in his pants and vest, was in his usual corner behind Josh and had not spoken all night.

"I know where there's a sick yin, and if it disnae get any help it's gonna die," Josh looked around the small group.

"Where is it. On the beach?" asked Angus.

"It's no important where it is. The thing that's important is what we can do about it." Josh felt a rush of adrenaline as the importance of his mission returned. He stepped into the middle of the bar and shouted for attention. To his question of whether or not there was a vet in the house there was a resounding silence. The clink of a glass being misplaced on a table and a coughing smoker reeling from a drag too far were the only response. There had been plenty of crushing moments in the past and there were sure to be plenty more in the future, so why should this feel any different? To Josh it did. Not only was it a night when he has been skinned alive in the drinking stakes by Stovey – a hitherto unheard of occurrence – but now he was behaving like a common or garden drunk pronouncing bollocks as closing time loomed. Crushed, he returned to his space at the bar, averting his eyes from Stovey's Cheshire cat grin. It was two minutes to midnight.

"So, what's it to be.... 'nother?" Stovey slurred as he fumbled loose change in his pocket, "cause I'm going in for number fourteen."

Stovey did indeed start his record-breaking fourteenth pint, but he didn't finish it. His liver hoisted the white flag before he had even downed the first quarter of the glass. His desperate lunge for the toilets was well timed, but when he resurfaced at the bar, eyes streaming and unsavoury stains covering the front of his yellow Ralph Lauren shirt, Tom Tom was far from happy and ordered him to sling his hook

Josh was also feeling queasy and decided to part company with The Gannet before his last pint was finished. Now he was regretting ever trying to catch up his drinking rival. Eight pints in less than half-an-hour was a dumb thing to do. Soon he found himself in a chip shop, which spun around him as a battered sausage and mushy peas were piled high in the poke of thick-cut chips. Then he was home. He stumbled through the front door and searched for the swing bin in the kitchen to deposit his chip wrappings. There was no one sitting up silently checking the clock, but still he tiptoed around, banging into cupboards that could have been avoided if he had been brave enough to switch on the room light. Habit stopped him from doing so, and it was habit that led him a trance-like walk to the living room where he flopped on the sofa and fell asleep.

At some stage during the night he flitted from the sofa to the bedroom and the comfort of the empty double bed, where he had not slept since the breakdown in love between himself and Suzy. There had been no conscious thought to go to the bedroom, it had been a primal instinct, as automatic as his drunken stagger home from the pub, a journey that had failed to register on his fuddled memory.

Now his head thumped with the unforgiving beat of a drummer boy's last stand. Groaning, he made his way to the bathroom. It was day, the light of morning bathed the house, but to Josh and his body it was still the middle of the night and the sooner he got to the toilet and relived his straining bladder, the sooner he could head back to bed and submit to the cranial hangover nightmare. The walls provided crucial support as he staggered and slouched to the bathroom. A twitch of movement in the bath water was evidence that the dolphin was there and alive.

"I've no forgotten aboot you. I jist huv to get ma heid straight first, ken," he offered as way of excuse for his sorry state.

It was his intention to sleep off the effects of last night until midday and then resume his search for help. There was no way he could envisage getting out of bed at an earlier moment. But how was he to know what was to happen that morning? How was he to know there would be a loud knock on the front door: a double rap, smart yet restrained, against the wood?

He groaned again in self pity and listened from the bed for the postman to shift the old wheelie bin from beside the front door and leave whatever the package was behind it, as he always did when any of Suzy's mail order catalogue purchases arrived. There was a second rap at the door, this time harder and with less patience.

"Leave it behind the bin," Josh shouted, but without much energy or projection. A third rap of the door, this time three loud bangs.

"Fuck's sake!" Naked, but for a pair of boxer shorts, he jumped up from the bed and went to the window, the curtains were still open from when Suzy had last touched them the morning she had walked out. He looked out. There had been times in his life when he had seen more police cars parked up outside, but at this immediate moment he couldn't recall any of those instances. He stared at a police van and three squad cars lined up against the pavement. An audience of Pinocchio-nosed neighbours had gathered in their gardens and at their front doors to watch the proceedings. He jumped back from the curtain, aware that he has been spotted by at least three of the police officers below. His jeans came to hand and he pulled them on, together with a t-shirt, as he hurried from the bedroom and crashed his way down the stairs, missing a few steps in his haste. The blood vessels in his head were pumping so hard he though they might burst.

What had he done at the pub last night? What had he done on the way home? If only he could remember. As he stood for a second at the bottom of the stairs he studied his hands; there were no cuts or bruises. He hasn't been fighting. So what did the police want?

The police, as it turned out, were the support act. Opening the front door a smidgen, blinking his eyes in the glare of a full-on assault by daylight, Josh was confronted by a man and woman. The man was big, both tall and wide, and his face was squashed beneath a blue Scottish Society for the Prevention of Cruelty to Animals cap. Josh did not pay much attention to the woman, who hovered in the background dressed in the same SSPCA navy blue uniform.

"Sir, are you the resident of this property?" the large man asked.

"Aye," Josh replied.

"We have reasons to believe you are keeping a sea mammal within these premises." The big man's stare bore down. Josh had figured out what has happened.

"The wee shite!" He remembered the boy at the bathroom window. He looked back at the bulky SSPCA man. "Sorry, I don't know what you're talking about," he said and moved to shut the door. Even as the door clicked into place there was a heavy knocking followed by further angry rapping.

The big SSPCA officer looked to his colleague standing to his left. "Difficult customer, as always."

The woman nodded, but she was almost in a trance. There was something about the man who opened the door that struck a cord of familiarity. She didn't get a good look at him during the brief exchange, but something about that snatched glimpse, that tone of voice, struck a chord inside her. One thing she could not mistake was the overpowering smell of stale beer on his breath. Even from a distance it had ignited a deep-seated trigger within her – a bad trigger. She stepped forward and rapped her knuckles against the door, almost battering her fist against the wood as thoughts of a low-life drunk harming a defenceless animal filled her mind.

"Look, I don't know who's sent youse, but you've got the wrang address," Josh shouted through the unopened door. His head reverberated with the banging, and he opened the door with an equally angry intensity. The woman SSPCA officer now stood in front of her heavy friend.

"Well, if you don't mind we'd like to check that out for ourselves," she said. Josh got his first clear look at her face.

"Katrina?" Somewhere in his addled brain an index card popped up. The face was familiar; her voice resonated. It had to be his old school friend.

"Josh. Josh Robertson?" she answered.

"What? I don't believe it. It's you," Josh opened the door wider without realising, as his eyes fixed on his one-time schoolgirl lover, his rebel-at-arms. "I didnae think I'd see you again after you moved doon to England. Whit are yi doing back here?"

Katrina raised her eyebrows playfully then flicked her gaze beyond him, over his shoulder and up the stairs. "Is there a lady of the house?"

"Was. She had enough of me," Josh tried to laugh. A wave of beer-breath swept across Katrina's nose and snapped her back to reality.

"Josh, we need to come in. It's in your own interest to let us carry out a check of the property."

The big guy behind Katrina impatiently shifted his weight from one foot to the other. Josh was aware that a number of the police officers hanging about on the street outside were gathering menacingly near the front gate.

His smile dropped. "Look, there's nowt here. Some snotty kid who called you – he's a right pain in the arse, he'll do anything to cause a bit of action in the street. Whit kind of story did he tell youse?"

"Can we come in and talk about it?" Katrina asked.

"Do you have to? It's a bit inconvenient."

Katrina nodded and looked over her shoulder at the three police officers at the gate, then she turned back to Josh.

"Do they have to come in as well?" Josh asked, his eyes peering over Katrina's shoulder at the police. The officers' faces also looked familiar to Josh, but that was no surprise as he knew most of the local division one way or another. He stepped back reluctantly and allowed Katrina across the threshold. The big SSPCA officer followed as if an invisible threat linked the two. The three police officers at the gate proceeded to walk down the path, when they reached the door Josh swung his arm across to block their way. "Sorry guys. Not enough room fur youse all."

The tall SSPCA officer hovered at the doorway as Katrina wandered into the living room, then the kitchen before returning to the front door. Her colleague now stood at the foot of the stairs. Josh was blocking the three police officers at the door.

"Your bathroom is upstairs?" Katrina asked, although it was less a question, more a statement.

"Top of the stairs," Josh replied deflated, realising the game was nearly up. Reassured that the police officers at the door were not going to enter the house, he followed Katrina up the stairs. Words were swimming around his mind as he tried to figure out a believable explanation for what was in the bath. As Katrina started to push open the bathroom door he began. "Katrina…" but his words dried up as the door opened and the blonde-haired woman stood there holding a red towel wrapped around her wet, dripping body.

Katrina froze as she took in the unexpected sight. "I'm sorry, I wasn't aware there was anyone else in the house," she apologised, reaching for the handle to close the door. She turned and faced Josh. "You should have told me there was someone having a bath."

"I…I thought she was still in bed," he replied. Katrina brushed past him and checked the remaining upstairs rooms.

"No woman of the house, eh?" she said under her breath as she returned to the top of the stairs where Josh remained beside the now closed bathroom door. She lifted her cap slightly to scratch her head. "Well, it appears we have been misinformed."

"I did try to tell you, but I suppose you've got a job to do."

Katrina was already making her way down the stairs to the front door, with Josh following close behind. She reached the doorway where her colleague stood with three bored looking police officers, then she turned and nodded to Josh. It was almost as though she no longer knew him. He was confused by her sudden change in attitude.

"It was nice seeing you again," he said. He watched as Katrina, the other SSPCA officer and the trio of police officers headed back out of the gate and into their respective cars before driving off one by one. Katrina's car was the last to depart. He saw her take one last, lingering look at him before speeding away. A few neighbours were still milling around outside, bemused by the lack of excitement and trying to weigh up the interlude's scandal value. Josh closed the front door.

"Did I create a problem?" the blonde-haired woman asked, coming down the stairs. She was wearing his jeans and a vibrant purple and green shirt that he had last worn when he was part of the nightclub scene as a twenty-something. Her blonde locks clashed alarmingly with the clothing's acid colour scheme.

"No, but if you'd been in the bath. Did you hear them arriving?"

She shook her head. Josh exhaled sharply. "Well." He paused as he tried to form the next word, then realised what was missing. "Well, we need to give you a name. Huv you got wan?"

She shook her head.

"Any suggestions?"

She shrugged.

"Well, I cannae call you dolphin. How aboot Doll? Nah, how about Dolly, that's a proper name," Josh smiled to himself, pleased with his spark of inspiration.

The feel-good factor lasted for most of the morning as he prepared a breakfast and then took Dolly to Ferry Bridge Road where they caught a bus to Cramond Beach.

It was Dolly's wish to return to the beach. Once they arrived at the footpath jetty leading down to the sand Josh let her lead the way. The cold waters of the Firth of Forth, seemingly forever warped by wind, stretched before them. Dolly's blonde hair flew around her head giving her the appearance of a demented water sprite as she called out to the water with a high trill cry that made Josh grab his ears fearing they might burst in the sonic frequency. He was twenty paces behind her and had no intention of following any further. Dolly strode ever closer to the water's edge until the lapping waves covered Suzy's walking boots. The colour drained from Josh's face. Suzy would throw a fit if she knew the murky waters of the Firth were right now tarnishing her proud boots. Every time she wore those hiking boots she made a point of cleaning them afterwards until they looked as immaculate as they had the day she'd paid the best part of one hundred pounds for them. Now they were being inundated by the salty water of the Firth, worn by a stranger whose feet were too small to hold them properly in place.

Dolly stopped walking. The boots vanished beneath the water that now lapped around her mid-calves, soaking into her. Her trill cry had stopped.

"Who are you trying to call?" Josh ventured. Dolly was listening, but not to Josh. She raised her left hand, gesturing for him to be quiet. Her attention remained focused on the water. For the next ten minutes she continued intermittently sending out a piercing trill cry and then listening to the silence that was enjoined only by the breeze coursing across the rippling water of the Firth. Josh was a picture of unease, he turned to look behind for signs of any people walking on the beach who might wonder what bizarre ritual he and the blonde-haired woman with the ill-fitting clothes were involved in. Finally his nerve gave in.

"We cannae stay oot here all day. We'll catch oor death fae the cold."

Dolly was inanimate, unmoved by either his words or the northerly breeze now pushing up off the water's surface stronger than ever as it lifted her hair like a ragged flag behind her head. Her head pitched forward a degree, the muscles of her neck showing the subtle strain. Her eyes were closed. A man with a black dog off its leash had strolled down the footpath from the main road and now stood at the end of the tarmac path, deciding which way to walk his pet. Josh could see him returning his stare.

"Go the other way," Josh whispered through gritted teeth. His psychic urging went straight over the head of the black dog, which did the exact opposite and padded straight towards him, unhindered by any unspoken human protocol about respecting a stranger's personal space. As sure as night follows day the obedient owner followed. The dog walker was a man in his fifties, a thick coat wrapped against the cold, one collar up and a black sea skipper's cap on his head to protect his thinning, grey hair. As he got closer, Josh turned his head back towards Dolly to hide his identity. The black dog circled him and moved to the water's edge, tasting the air around Dolly in a puzzled manner.

"Samson, come here," growled the dog walker, his pet ran back to him, kicking up tufts of wet sand.

Dolly had stopped calling. She retreated from the water, Suzy's boots squelching with each step as she approached Josh.

"There is not much time," she said solemnly.

"For what?"

"If I'm to get back with the others. They are leaving on the night of the full moon. They can not wait any longer or they risk missing the currents and the chance to join with the main group."

"The others? What, other dolphins?"

Dolly nodded. Her eyes were staring at the ground and she looked as though she was about to cry.

"You've spoken to them? Was that the high-pitch stuff?"

Dolly appeared not to have heard his question, or had chosen to ignore it. "I need your help."

"What?" Josh had tucked his hands into his trouser pockets to protect them from the northerly breeze that now rushed harder. "Why can't you go back in the waater now? If your friends are oot there why no join them right noo? They'll help yi."

Dolly shook her head. "I'd be a burden. I can't see in the water with my sonic ability impaired. I'd be losing my way all the time. I need to cure myself of this…whatever this curse is."

Josh sighed. "So, how long before the next full moon?"

"Four sunrises." Dolly's answer barely registered when Josh began to feel a headache coming on. The pain grew into a persistent throb as he and Dolly turned in silence to depart from the beach. Up ahead was the man with the black dog. They caught up and passed him without exchanging any words. The silence continued as Dolly and Josh walked to the shelter and caught a bus heading back into the city. It was nearly lunchtime and Josh's head was spinning as he tried to figure out his next move. Then things got worse.

"We need to get off." Dolly was insistent, grabbing Josh's right arm so tightly that even beneath the thickness of his jacket he felt her fingers pinch his skin.

"We've still another stop to go," he pulled his arm free.

"I can't keep this form any longer. I'm changing," Dolly whispered urgently. Josh swiveled to see if anyone else on the top of the double decker bus had heard. There were two other passengers, an elderly man and a young teenager who was wearing headphones from an unseen personal music player that created a hornet's nest buzz around his head. He was seated four rows away, the old man was sitting further back.

Josh turned to Dolly. "Fuck, you're joking?" he mumbled. There was no need for her to reply, for he could see the lustre of her skin changing. The healthy pink glow had faded to take on a pale grey-blue tinge. Her blue eyes had lost their sparkle and become darker.

"You cannae change into a dolphin. No on a bus," Josh insisted, trying to smother his increasingly incredulous words as he snatched another frantic glance backwards. Neither of the other two top deck passengers appeared to have noticed anything out of the ordinary was taking place.

"I need water. I need to have water to stop." Dolly's breathing was strained and shallow, sounding like an asthma patient or a heart attack victim fighting for life.

"Water?" Josh jumped to his feet and rang the stop bell.

≈

When the doors of The Gannet crashed open, Tom Tom the bartender could barely hide his surprise as Josh hurried in with the blonde-haired woman. The woman's pale, sickly complexion worried him immediately, he also did a double take of the clock on the wall, it had barely turned noon and Josh had always been more of a late afternoon and evening drinker. "She all right?" he inquired as Josh and the woman lurched towards the bar.

"Aye, she's fine. Give us some bottles of waater."

"Waater?"

"Aye, you ken, mineral waater. You do serve it don't you?" Josh could not conceal his panic.

"How many? Two?"

"Four."

Four plastic bottles of mineral water, minus their tops, were duly placed on the bar counter in front of Josh, who waved a five pound note in the air before placing it on the counter and taking the bottles in one hand, spaced between his stretched fingers. With his other arm still holding Dolly upright he guided her to the far corner of the pub. There were four lunchtime drinkers sitting close to one another beside the door. They watched the progress of the newcomers until they had found their seats then turned back to renew their hushed conversation above their table of pints.

Dolly drank all four bottles in quick succession. The trembling of her body subsided noticeably, but her pale skin remained almost ghost-like, a beacon shining in the dim corner of the pub.

"Is that enough?" Josh asked, eyes wide with concern. Dolly shook her head. Tom Tom had lined up two more bottles at the counter and was keeping a close watch on the unusual customer and her ferocious thirst. Josh left her for a moment to return to the bar to collect the next round of mineral waters.

"She's got a bit of a thirst on her. Where you been, out jogging or summit?" Tom Tom asked.

"Make it four," Josh nodded towards the mineral water bottles and fumbled in the front pockets of his trousers, fishing out a crumpled tenner.

There were fourteen empty water bottles cluttered on the small pub table before Dolly nodded her head and sighed with quiet relief. Josh collapsed backwards against his seat and took in the view of the discoloured, off-white ceiling.

"You stopping for a pint then, Josh?" Tom Tom was hovering above him as he collected some of the empties from the table. "Might as well, eh. The others'll be here in a minute."

The blood in Josh's feet froze and he looked at the partially cleared table, still littered with almost a dozen mineral water bottles. What a travesty. If Stovey or Angus saw this he'd be the laughing stock. Mineral water, eh….not even cola. He snapped back to life. "Nah, I've got to get this yin back hame before she has another turn," he replied.

"Josh….is that you, Josh?" Not even the words of a hangman on the gallows could have struck deeper into Josh's soul. He waited for the questioner to appear from behind the corner, and as he did so he wrapped his arms around the remaining bottles on the table in a desperate effort to hide the evidence, but it was too late, there he stood before him.

"Peter," Josh's arms went limp, releasing the bottles. In front of the table stood Blind Peter, barely clothed as always.

"It's no like you to be drinking in the daytime. Whit's the matter wi yi?" Peter asked.

"Nowt, honest. I'm jist getting a drink for a friend and I wis leaving."

Tom Tom intervened to the side with a barely concealed snigger. "I'll clear these bottles," he said as he reached down to lift the remaining empties from the table.

"Bottles? You're drinking bottles? I thought you said people who drink fae bottles were softies?" Blind Peter observed. Josh accidentally brushed against him as he stood up and led Dolly from the table. He did not answer his friend; there would be time to discuss niceties later.

"Hey, Josh. You want to take that jacket hame that you left last night?" Tom Tom held up the leather jacket. It was damp from beer spills and from having lain in a musty corner of the pub since he had forgotten it in his sozzled 'anyone know a vet' state as he departed The Gannet the night before. Now Josh brandished the jacket like a cloak, placing it around Dolly's shoulders as he hustled her outside.

Despite the smell of stale beer on the jacket, a perfume air danced around Dolly and dreamily filled Josh's senses. He felt he was floating, which was a not altogether unique sensation as he walked from The Gannet, but this time it had a different quality as he retreated from the pub. Dolly's hair was lifted gently by the breeze and brushed softly against his cheek as he supported her and matched her elegant footfalls. Nothing was said as they wandered back through the streets and alleys. It was one of those awkward times Josh had become used to in his life – a time when his mind blanked out all thoughts so completely that he could think of nothing relevant to say. It wasn't until they were in sight of the house that Dolly, still wrapped beneath the drink-stained jacket, spoke. She was shaking as though cold, and her skin was waning, leaking colour and texture once more.

"I need water. It is too much for me to keep this form so long. I...I don't know how much longer I can do this. It might be better for me to remain in my true form," she said.

With one arm around her waist, Josh hurried her the final steps to the house. He hastily unlocked the door, he didn't want to have a dolphin in his arm in the street, not with the twitching net curtains and stool pigeon kids lurking. All the same, he felt he was being watched. He was right. Further along the street an old blue car, rusting badly around its sills, was parked tightly against the curb on the opposite side of the road. There were two woman occupants, both monitoring his progress with Dolly. Suzy was sitting in the front passenger seat; her eyes were red through hours of crying over the past days. Beside her was Maxine, her closest friend at school and the nearest thing she had to a sister.

"He's still with her," Suzy choked back her sadness as she watched Josh and Dolly holding on to one another.

"What does he see in her? She looks a mess," Maxine pronounced, straining her eyes to see the blonde-haired Dolly.

Suzy sniffled. Her red-ringed eyes stared out at the distant couple. Maxine reached across and touched Suzy's right hand, where it rested on her lap.

"I've got to confront him – and her," Suzy wiped her eyes and watched as Josh led the woman up the garden path to the front door.

Maxine nodded, then noticed a red car turn onto the street, drive past them and pull up outside the house. "Hold on, who's that then?"

CHAPTER TEN

CATCHING UP

Josh closed the front door behind him. The house was cold and lifeless. Without Suzy, none of the housework had been done for days, the heating had been switched off in all that time and it was only now, as he began to shiver, that he noticed. He picked up his beer-soaked jacket from the hallway floor where Dolly had unceremoniously discarded it as she rushed up the stairs to the bathroom. He placed it on his shoulders and made his way to the kitchen to switch on the immersion heater.

"I'll put the heating on. It's like an ice cube in here," he called up to Dolly. He hadn't seen the blue car further along the street, from where Suzy and Maxine had spied, nor had he seen the smart red car turning into the road as he reached the front door. But now its driver was banging on the front door.

"Whit now?" he called out. Through the frosted glass he could see the outline of someone dressed in dark clothing and wearing a cap. He wondered if it was a police officer.

"What do you want?" he asked as he approached the door.

"Can you open the door? There's something I need to ask you and I'd rather not do it from the street." Josh recognised the soft voice and quickly swung the door open. Standing at the step was Katrina, still wearing her SSPCA uniform.

"Katrina," Josh said half in surprise, half in delight.

"I'm sorry to disturb you again but," Katrina stopped. Josh was no longer looking at her, but was instead poking his head out of the door and flicking a glance up and down the road. He retracted his neck.

"Not brought your buddies along this time?" he noted.

"Look, I want to apologise for what happened. We had a report, two reports actually, and we had to come and check them out."

Josh stuffed his hands in the front pockets of his jeans and listened.

"It's been such a long time since we've seen one another – we haven't spoken since school," Katrina continued.

"Is this a social call or are you still nosing around?" Josh remained sharp, trying to hide a growing delight at seeing his old friend. Katrina, brought up short by his comment, dropped her eyes and looked at Josh's worn brown shoes. Some things, it seemed, never change. She looked up and into his eyes. Where were the words now that she needed them to answer back? She let her mind settle and balance.

"If that's what you think...."

"Sure, that's what I think," Josh rolled on. "What do you expect me to think? Snooping around on the say-so of some gobshite. Jeez, as if I'd be keeping a dolphin in my bathroom. What were you thinking, Katrina? You used to be so smart. Has that cap gone to your head?"

Katrina felt anger rising in her. "I was doing my job. I came to apologise. I thought you'd understand." She barely finished the sentence before she turned to walk away. She had intended to make a slow retreat, but instead found herself walking almost twice as fast as normal towards the gate and the miserable street beyond.

Josh bowed his head for a moment then snapped it back and called after her. "Wait. I'm no angry with you. Look...do you want a cup of tea?"

Katrina stopped, her left hand resting lightly on the top of the open wooden gate at her side as she weighed the invite. The street pavement was a single step away. Slowly she turned and faced him.

Josh remained still, trying to gauge her intention. She slowly stepped forward and returned to the door, standing less than a foot from Josh.

"Tea? Aye," she smiled, her words were bedded in the comforting tones once shared between the pair in their school days. Josh returned the smile. He stepped aside to let her in.

Katrina stood at the foot of the stairs and looked around the silent surroundings.

"So, what's the story?" she asked.

Josh followed her eyes as she looked around at the walls and the ceiling. "What, this? There's no much to tell. First tell me aboot you. Where huv you been all this time?"

"Married. Divorced," Katrina replied.

"Who to?"

"Bobby. No one you know. He couldn't climb out of the alcoholic pit he'd fallen into. I tried to pull him out."

Josh nodded slowly. Katrina continued, but it was as though she was now talking about a third party, divorcing herself from herself as she recalled the adult events of her life.

"They said we had a perfect relationship. He was a draftsman with one of the best companies and I was an up-and-coming marine specialist officer. When I walked down the aisle I'd never been happier. We were both 24 and on the verge of golden careers."

She smiled, but avoided direct eye contact with Josh. "The life I'd promised myself was coming true. My studies were complete; I was qualified. My dedication had not gone unnoticed. I was promoted almost every year."

Josh watched her eyes move from one side to the other as she reached into her mind for clarity. Her smile slipped and was replaced with a look of anxiety and worry.

"My success was in direct contrast to Bobby's deterioration."

"Booze?" Josh gulped.

"Aye," Katrina replied. "Even before we were married he had always enjoyed a drink with 'the boys'. We met at university and for the first year of our marriage the newness of it all and our busy lives masked Bobby's drinking, but it had grown with each lunchtime session. At first I had thought it was a bonding phase, which would settle down as he became established at work. Then on our first anniversary he did not come home until the next day, almost comatose from a weekend binge."

"Tea," Josh remembered his offer and led the way to the kitchen. With the kettle on he turned to Katrina and noticed her eyes, she seemed to be in a trance, retrieving her memories.

"I'd never seen Bobby in such a state – but it soon became his natural way. He drank his livelihood every night until he was unable to wake in the mornings for work. There were enough friendly warnings, then written reprimands and finally he was asked to resign."

Josh interjected. "So you called it a day, told him to sling his hook?"

Katrina almost snapped back into the present, but not quite. "We struggled on. I had a big increase in my salary. But Bobby sank into a drinking morose which sucked out his will to find work. His rages and outbursts were savage. I ended up in hospital."

"What?"

"More than once. After the third time I couldn't kid myself any more so I started divorce proceedings. He left and went to live with his drinking buddies, dossing down in some charity hostel. I sold the house and returned to Scotland."

She became silent as she contemplated what she had said. She had drunk alcohol herself, mostly wine, but now she could not bring herself to touch a drop. Even the smell of liquor was enough to set her on edge. She despised alcohol in all its forms and could not stand alcoholics; she detested them as much as she detested those she prosecuted for animal cruelty. An involuntary shiver passed through her body. She took the warm cup of tea Josh offered and cradled it with both hands.

"And you?" she looked at Josh.

"Me?"

"Aye, what's your story?"

Josh smiled, but it was a short-lived smile. A loud splash from the upstairs bathroom and an unmistakable high-pitched squeak interrupted the moment. Katrina's startled eyes widened.

CHAPTER ELEVEN

RUN AN ERRAND

For a moment Josh said nothing, but fear was written large across his face. His eyes were alive with panic. The sound of more high-pitched squeaking and splashing drifted down from the bathroom again. He looked upwards then back at Katrina's quizzical face.

"There's something I need to tell you," he was almost breathless with tension. "Can you keep a secret?"

"Josh, don't do this to me. You know who I am," Katrina flicked her eyes towards her cap then back at him.

"I need your help," he pleaded.

"There's a dolphin up there, right?" Katrina concluded.

Josh nodded.

"Just like we were told?"

He nodded again.

With her senses fully alert Katrina picked out the smell of stale alcohol permeating from the leather jacket slung over Josh's shoulder. It reeked of beer as though it had been used as a mop to soak up spillage, strangely enough a thought that had also crossed Josh's mind earlier. The heavy stench of alcohol triggered her distaste for drunkards. The shutters came down.

"You were drunk and you brought a dolphin into your house," she put the jigsaw pieces together.

"Sort of," Josh began. "Look, can we go into the living room and talk for a moment," he gestured with his hand towards the front room then winced as the dolphin squeaked again. Katrina followed his desperate invite. It was mid-afternoon but the curtains were still drawn; Josh made no attempt to open them, opting instead to switch on the light. Katrina watched him intently. She perched on the edge of an armchair.

"Do you remember the time when we were at school?" Josh asked.

"Any specific time?" Katrina's tone verged on mocking.

"When we used to skip school and go doon the beach."

Katrina nodded.

"That time we found those lads laying into the wee dolphin on the sand. Remember that?"

"Yes, Josh you're not going to say what I think you're going to say?"

"And what's that?"

"That the dolphin upstairs is the same one."

He nodded. "Aye, exactly."

"Josh, are you out of your mind?"

Josh took two steps towards her, his eyes pleading. "That dolphin, the one those boys were kicking. That's the one upstairs in the bathroom and it needs help again, it's got some kind of," but he was unable to finish his sentence.

Katrina was on her feet and trying to distance herself. "You're mad, or drunk."

"Listen to me," Josh stretched out to touch her arm, but instantly wished he hadn't as she flinched and pulled away, shaking her head.

"Katrina, you have to trust me on this." He shut up and looked at her; she stood halfway towards the door, facing away. He wondered what she was thinking and waited for her to speak, but as the silence grew longer he caved in and broke the pregnant pause. "What are you going to do?"

Katrina half turned. "You know my job. You can't keep a dolphin in your house. I'll have to call my office." She reached into her brown shoulder bag and fished out a mobile phone. Josh snatched it.

"No, not yet. Katrina, I want this dolphin to go back into the sea. But you've got to help me make it better."

Katrina held out her hand. "Give me the phone."

"Are you going to call someone?"

"Give me the phone."

"Will you come and look at the dolphin?"

"Josh – the phone."

He relented and passed the mobile phone back, but only half released his grip so that Katrina had to apply force to free it from his grasp. Katrina stood motionless for a moment, looking at the phone in her hand and poised to make a call until she closed her hand fully around it and placed it back in her bag.

"Okay, show me," she said. Josh released the breath he was holding and led her upstairs to the bathroom where the dolphin was sprawled the full length of the bathtub. The near overflowing water was lapping on the lip of the tub as the creature lifted its beak half upwards and out of the water. Katrina gasped.

"I don't believe it. How did you carry this thing all the way from the beach without killing it?" Her words were riveted with deep concern.

"It's a long story."

"I'll bet." Katrina knelt and stroked the dolphin's wet skin, staring at the gentle eye at the side of its head that looked back at her. She recognised it as a common dolphin, a resident of the North Sea and western coasts of the United Kingdom. Although an adult, the dolphin was relatively small and had been scarred by rocks and nets. There was a striking cut along the edge of its back indicating it had, at some point, fallen victim to the propellers of a boat.

"Can you see whit's wrang?" Josh asked, bending over slightly as Katrina continued to run one hand along the dolphin's body.

She shook her head. She felt nervous and unsettled and needed time to think. "I'll need to do a few tests first, if it is a virus. There's no way of knowing just by looking and certainly not when it's confined to such a small space," she chided.

"You can't take her away."

"Her?" Katrina looked up. "Josh, this dolphin is going to die if you leave it in here. It needs space to move around."

"She cannae be moved," Josh was adamant. "I know whit's wrang way her. It's a virus that's affecting her sonar. There's something oot in the waater that's caused it. Katrina, you must have come across something like this before. All she needs is some medicine and then we can release her back into the sea."

As he spoke, Katrina stood up and faced him squarely. "How are you so sure about all that?"

"I jist know. Trust me."

Katrina shook her head. She sensed something was seriously amiss.

"Is there some medicine you give to dolphins that have a virus?" Josh continued.

"Yes, there is," she replied. "But we need to run tests first to find out for sure what is ailing it."

"Then you'll have to run the tests here."

Katrina looked at him, allowing his words to hang in the air for a moment. She turned back to the dolphin in the bathtub and knelt once more beside it, this time leaning closer. The dolphin emitted a high-pitched squeak and Katrina held its mouth open slightly, examining inside.

"You've come across this before?" Urgency bolted through Josh's words.

"I'm familiar with the virus most commonly picked up by dolphins and porpoise in our coastal waters. This looks like it might be the same thing." Katrina sat back on her heels, lifting her cap and sweeping her now wet right hand through her long, black hair.

"Then you ken whit to do," Josh surmised.

"Josh, we get called out to cats and dogs and rabbits. We're not a dolphin agency. That's an area for the crustacean rescue folk."

"Don't say that, Katrina. You said yourself you were a marine specialist. We've got to do something. We've only got four days."

"What?" Katrina stood up.

"We need to get her back in the sea in next three days or she'll be left behind by the others," Josh explained

"What are you talking about. What others?"

"Her family, her group. They swim together. She needs to join them before they leave the Firth." He could see his words were flying over her head, which she was nervously shaking again.

"How do you know this?"

"She...I...I just dae. You've got tae trust me."

The dolphin squeaked and a flipper splashed water over the edge of the bathtub against Katrina's leg. Instinctively she moved a step to the side.

"I don't want to know," Katrina waved her hands at him. "My priority is getting this dolphin back into the sea where it belongs."

"Making her better first," Josh added.

"Yes." Katrina stared down at the dolphin as she collected her thoughts. She needed to piece together what was really going on, and to do that she needed to get Josh away from the dolphin, away from the house.

Josh was eager for the next move and bit his tongue as long as he could, which turned out to be just less than 23 seconds. "So?" he blurted.

"You'll have to fetch some things for me." Katrina took a pen from her bag and wrote down an address on a scrap of paper, handing it to him. "This is my office."

"That's the other side of town. I'm gonna need to take your car."

"No," Katrina shot back. "I'll need it if things deteriorate. The bus will be as quick."

"Are you guising? The bus?" Josh was incredulous at the suggestion, which sounded like instructing an astronaut to take a microlight to the moon.

"An hour at the outside and you'll be there and back."

Josh pulled his neck in sharply. "Well, if you says so. Will they give me the stuff like?"

"Yes. I'll call ahead on my mobile and tell them what I need and that you're collecting."

"Dae it now before I go in case there's a problem," Josh said.

Katrina shook her head. "You get going and I'll call as soon as I've decided exactly what I'm going to require. Go on, shoo," she said.

They both descended the stairs and stood for a moment in the hallway before Josh opened the front door and stepped outside. Katrina stepped half outside and planted an unexpected kiss on his cheek. Josh felts the years roll back.

"Now go, and hurry up if you want to save this dolphin," Katrina commanded and shoed him gently away with her hands. Josh half stumbled backwards and then turned and quickly made his way up the short garden path and out the gate on to the pavement. He glanced back once more to see Katrina still at the door watching him depart, and then he focused on the street ahead and his own mission, breaking into a half jog along the pavement as he navigated his way out of the housing scheme to the nearest bus stop.

Still sitting in the rusty blue car further along the street, Suzy and Maxine had watched Josh emerge from the house. They had watched as he turned back and was kissed by the SSPCA woman standing at the door, and they had watched as he made his hurried departure along the pavement while the SSPCA woman went back inside and closed the door. Suzy was dumbstruck, unable to form any words as her eyes widened. She took in everything, but made sense of none of it.

"What the....what's going on?" She finally managed to ask.

"Quite a ladies' man. He works fast....you never told me," then Maxine realised her words were not helping and she fell silent. Suzy was already fidgeting with the handle and swung the passenger door open.

"Hey, where you going?" Maxine called.

"To find out exactly what's going on." Suzy stormed purposefully down the street at a half jog. Josh was also at a half jog, heading in the opposite direction, oblivious to what was unfolding behind. He vanished around the corner while Suzy bore down on the house. Maxine stood next to the car, the driver's door resting against her thigh, one arm bent against the roof as she watched Suzy closing in on the house.

Katrina was standing in the hallway making a call on her mobile phone when she was startled by the sound of heavy knocking on the front door. "Okay, I've got to go, I'll call you right back," she ended the conversation in a half-whisper, dropped the phone into her handbag and opened the door, expecting to see Josh.

"So what did you forget?" but her question fell flat as she came face to face with a distressed looking woman with ruffled peroxide blonde hair.

"Who are you?" Suzy barely suppressed her anger.

"Sorry?" Katrina snapped out of a momentary daze.

"Who are you?" Suzy repeated. "And what are you doing here?"

"I'm with the SSPCA, I'm investigating a call. Who you are?"

"I live here." Suzy folded her arms.

"*You* live here? But I saw Mr Robertson's partner this morning. Are you sure you're at the right house?"

"Oh yes. I'm quite sure. I left a few days ago. Now I'm back to see what's going on. What were you doing kissing him? Is that part of your job?"

"We're old friends, from way back," said Katrina. She noticed Suzy's eyes widen and quickly added, "From going to school together. We haven't seen one another since then."

A scowl was fixed on Suzy's face. "So what about the other women he's got in here?"

Katrina looked over her shoulder back into the house then returned her attention to Suzy. "I ... I really don't know. Look, if you're who you say you are then we need to talk."

From a distance Maxine watched the doorstep exchange, she tried to judge what was going on. Then Suzy entered the house and the door closed. Maxine sighed and sat back inside the car, closing the door only enough so it half clicked into place. She stared out through the windscreen at the pale grey landscape of the housing estate, and waited.

≈

Josh knew nothing of the drama he'd left behind. Despite his ungainly jog he made good progress winding his way through the streets towards The Gannet and the main bus route. Pulling the piece of paper from his pocket, he looked at the address Katrina had scribbled. To reach it he would have to go through the centre of town and out to the other side. As he feared, the bus driver told him he needed to change on Princes Street for a number 32. He made his way to the front of the top deck and watched the city unravel around him. Silently – and some times not so silently – he cursed as the bus seemed to halt at every stop to let passengers on or off. He felt a growing desire to shout something to the driver to urge him on. The clock was ticking.

By the time the tall Georgian buildings of the city centre blocked the view from the top of the bus it was nearly half an hour since he had boarded. Princes Street was nearby.

"An hour there and back, my arse," he swore to himself as he checked his watch. The grey pall of clouds hanging over the city dampened the spirits of shoppers crowding the pavements, suppressing the colours of the gardens and adding a grim light to the foreboding rocky features of the castle, sitting like a cork on top of the town.

"You'll catch the 32 up the other end of the street," the driver instructed as Josh disembarked.

"The other end?"

The driver nodded without looking, instead flicking his eyes to his rear view mirror.

"That's the other end of Princes Street. Are you no going any closer?" Josh contemplated the mile-long walk.

"Sorry pal. I turn aff here."

Josh jumped down the final step from the bus and scanned the bobbing heads of the shoppers filling the pavements along the busy shopping street, the other end of which was out of sight and shrouded in a grey that was a mixture of rain and mist, or as Josh called it 'glum'. There was no way he would get to his destination in the half-hour forecast. He needed to call Katrina and tell her about the delay, but the only mobile phone he'd ever owned, 'a true Stovey special', had died on him a month ago. He searched around and saw a phone box. Pulling open the dirty door to get inside, he picked up the receiver to dial home, but all he heard was the silence of a dead line. He slammed down the handset, almost shattering its dated, black plastic coating and stormed out of the phone box into the heaving throng of mid-afternoon shoppers, tripping over the low swinging bags of heavily laden old women and dawdling tourists. It couldn't get any worse, he thought.

"It's worse," he corrected, cursing as he caught sight of the row of bus stops ahead and saw a claret-coloured double-decker pulling away, the number 32 emblazoned in mocking day-glow green in the rear destination screen. "Shit!" he punched the Perspex encased timetable attached to the bus stop pole. An hour had almost gone and he was only halfway there. If he was frustrated at that moment, his frustration multiplied when it seemed that two of every other bus number pulled in at the stop and drove off before another number 32 finally showed up. Jumping aboard he showed the scrap of paper to the driver.

"Dae yi ken where this is?" he asked. The driver nodded. "Gee us a shout when we git there?" and Josh bumped along the aisle to find a seat. The driver was as good as his word, and after what seemed like an aeon of passing through dull estates that looked no different than the one from which Josh had come, the driver called out as the bus reached the furthest outpost on its route before doubling back and heading for the city centre. As the bus slowed Josh was not impressed by what he saw outside the window. It was the outskirts of yet another housing scheme with barely a shop or office in sight.

"Are yi sure this is it?" he asked as he stood up.

"There's the road sign right there," the driver pointed at a half vandalised street sign screwed onto a low wall near the bus stop. It was indeed the same road as the one that Katrina had scrawled down on the piece of paper. All the same, Josh found it hard to believe the offices of the SSPCA were to be found in this rundown locale. He alighted from the bus and stood and stared at the fag end of the nondescript housing estate. The only sound was the dull rumbling of the departing bus, which soon faded away. All around were gardens with wild, knee-high grass where lawns might once have been. Cheap, plastic wire fences were twisted and pulled down, stretched and contorted by the uncaring hands of youths crisscrossing people's back and front gardens to create crappy shortcuts to nowhere. Most of the ground floor windows of the semi-detached council houses were boarded up and covered in mostly unintelligible graffiti, although the word 'Fuck' stood out boldly in white emulsion on one board.

"This is a bigger shit hole than oor bit," Josh commented, although there was no one on the street to hear him. He booted a crushed can of Younger's Tartan Bitter out of his path and listened to it clatter against the pavement's cracked and broken concrete before it slid off the kerb and into the gutter.

He began to walk, but his inner voice was already running a pissed-off commentary. There was no SSPCA office here – no one would open an office in this scummy neighbourhood, where even the cobalt grey sky looked depressed to be associated with the place. Yet, as the narrative spilled out across his mind, Josh was compelled to carry on, scanning the scrap of paper as he strolled forward with purpose, the anger boiling in his body as he counted off the house numbers until he reached number 90. This was it, and it was a rotten house just like all the others. The garden was marginally maintained, and the fence was still in one piece, but there was no way it was anything other than an ordinary house. He walked up the path and knocked.

"Aye?" the small, middle-aged woman of the house asked as she opened the door.

"Is this the SSPCA?" Josh fired straight away, but with little conviction that he was going to get the answer he wanted.

"You whit?"

"Some one telt me that this was the SSPCA."

The woman was no longer engaged with Josh and instead had turned away and was heading back into the house. "Doug, come here." She returned and stood silently looking at Josh. Behind her came the mumbled noise of someone complaining, and then approaching footsteps. A big man appeared wearing a filthy pair of jeans and a string vest strained across his bulging belly. His bare arms were thick and heavily tattooed. The fellow was as big as Angus, and his face bore the signs of an old glassing from a pub brawl.

Josh backed away. "I can see I've got the wrang place. I've got to run, cheers."

"You whit?" the hulk shouted, though he had no need to as Josh was still only a few feet away. His mousy wife said something, mentioning the SSPCA.

The big man stared hard at Josh. "Are you taking the piss?"

Now Doug was coming out of the house in his bare, black-toed feet. Josh backed further away and walked at double speed out of the gate, his body half-turned in the direction of Doug and the open door of the house.

"Want yir face smashed?" Doug's bulging arms tensed as he marched down the path to the gate. Josh no longer looked behind. He was back on the pavement and running. It wasn't until he was out of the street and around the next corner that he dared look over his shoulder. He wasn't being chased. A bus stop was up ahead and he made his way to it, catching his breath.

By the time he got off his fourth bus of the day, near The Gannett, the entire excursion had taken him almost three hours. He was mightily pissed off and his feet ached. He walked past The Gannet without so much as a sideways glance. Storming along he was soon in his home street again, his house four doors away. There was no one around except a street kid kicking a ball against the next-door neighbour's wooden garden fence. As Josh approached, the youngster stopped kicking the ball.

"They've taken your dolphin away, mister," said the boy.

CHAPTER TWELVE

A CONFRONTATION

"Katrina!" Josh yelled as he flung open the door and dashed through the living room and kitchen. The place had been turned upside down. For a moment he stared at the upturned drawers, the bills and letters scattered across the floor beside the writing bureau in the corner of the living room. The drinks cabinet has been emptied, the bottles left lying in a group nearby.

He called out again as he returned to the hallway, kicking the front door shut with his boot and launching himself up the stairs to the bathroom. There was water all over the floor, pooling in the uneven linoleum. The bath was still half full of cold water.

In the afternoon light he could see the water trail leading from the bathroom to the landing carpet and then down the stairs towards the front door.

"Shit!" His boot landed on the skirting board, embedding itself in the off-white paintwork. The bedroom had been untidily searched. His and Suzy's clothes were piled on the bed. All the drawers had been opened. A bookshelf had been disturbed, and Suzy's paperback pulp romances replaced in a haphazard fashion with all their spines brutally broken. Josh collapsed on the bed among the displaced clothes and coat hangers and stared at the ceiling.

There was a heavy rap on the front door. With angry adrenaline still flooding his body, he jumped to his feet and ran to the top of the stairs then crouched down to spy the shadow against the frosted glass. There were two shadows. A gloved hand banged against the door again.

"Mr Robertson," a police officer called.

Josh bounded down the stairs and threw open the door. "Aye." He shot a piercing stare at the two officers on the doorstep. They were big men, and standing further back, lingering next to the gate, was a third officer. Josh knew they are not leaving without him.

"We'd like you to escort us to the station," said one of the two at the doorstep.

"Why, whit's up, feart someone is gonna beat youse up?" Josh delivered with sarcasm. The police officers glanced nervously at one another.

"Youse are the guisers who thrashed this place, is that no right?" Josh continued. It was less a question, more an accusation. There was a dark smile on his face as he nodded slowly at the silent officers. "No trouble yi to move your buckies a bit mare and tidy up afterwards, ken what I mean?"

"Mr Robertson, are you going to come with us or not?" the same officer asked again.

"Whit are my options?" He knew the answer. He was steamed having seen his home ripped up and the dolphin gone. He wanted to know where Dolly was.

Walking into a police station voluntarily was a lifetime first for Josh, but he sensed he'd not be walking back out a free man. The corridor walls were washed-out blue, the type of blue that couldn't make its mind up whether to be blue or fade to grey. There was a black border running six inches along the skirting and the same distance around the top of the wall before the white ceiling took over, reflecting the dazzle of the constantly switched on strip lighting. The whole set-up smacked of a battery hen farm.

"I know what you're thinking," the duty sergeant said as he led Josh along the corridor to interview room four.

"Oh aye," Josh replied.

"That this place smacks of a battery hen farm."

"Eh?"

The sergeant smiled as he shut the door of the interview room behind Josh and pointed to the white plastic chair in front of the table at the centre of the sparse, sound-proofed room. "It's what you said the last time you were in here."

Josh scratched his chin and tried to recall the face of the duty sergeant, but he was familiar with so many of the coppers in this district of the city it was difficult to pull individual faces and names out of his memory at will. He flopped onto the chair like an overgrown schoolboy eager to show defiance to a grown-up.

"Gonna tell me whit this is all aboot?" he asked.

The sergeant sat at the opposite side of the table and stared at Josh for a moment. "Dolphin," he said, deadpan.

For a moment Josh remained silent and waited. Then he waited some more, and then still some more. "Is this some kind of word game?" he finally replied.

"No Josh, this isnae a game. You had a dolphin in your bath and you shouldn't have. Care to explain?"

"That disnae gie you the right to break-in to ma hoose and turn it into a shit hole."

"Turn it *into* a shit hole?" the sergeant repeated with mock incredulity.

"What were you looking fur, mare dolphins in the wardrobe?"

"The woman from the SSPCA let us in. You let her in. There wisnae any break-in," said the sergeant.

"That's whit you say, but it'll no stand up in front of the judge and you ken that," Josh was feeling where the conversation was going.

The sergeant pulled back and folded his arms. "Well, we can arrange to test that theory."

"Is this why I've had to come here? So you can tell me that you took the dolphin away?"

"It's an offence."

"So why don't you arrest me?" Josh offered his wrists across the table.

The sergeant sniffed, but kept his arms folded. "Before I dae that, I want you to admit you let us search your property."

"Have you got a blood clot in your heed. Think I'm a bampot? Youse were oot of order and now you're brickin' it. Serves youse right for going aff half-cocked as usual." Now it was Josh's turn to sit back in his plastic chair with his arms folded and a smug grin on his face.

"Don't arse aboot. Having a dolphin in your bath isnae a stroll in the park. You'll get time for this, trust me. On top of the theft of the carpet, it won't sit very pretty," the sergeant's eyes were flaming.

"So, I get time."

"Or you say you let us come in and retrieve the dolphin and we lessen the punishment."

Now the picture was materialising. The barter was on the table. The plods had overstepped the mark, entering and searching without a warrant. Their collective arses were on the line too. Josh let the sergeant squirm in silence as he totted up his bargaining chips. Giving the clink a body swerve was a potent offer, but maybe there was an even better deal to be had.

"What say you drop everything and I say nowt aboot your wee visit?"

The sergeant shook his head slowly. "Can't do that. There's other agencies involved."

"Then it looks like you're really up shit creek."

"Come on Josh. You don't want to do time for something like this."

Josh considered. He was still considering the proposition an hour later after he had walked from custody. He had signed a statement that said he had invited the police into his home to liberate the dolphin from his bath and, in return, he had been spared a visit to a jail cell.

He was warned a charge might follow later. Quite why he had put his trust in the fuzz he wasn't sure. The urge had been to make life as difficult as possible for his sworn adversaries, but now there was something greater driving him on. He could feel it gripping his stomach, tightening his muscles like a deep-seated need that had to be satisfied.

A street away from the police station was a charity shop, run for the benefit of the SSPCA. Josh went in and asked for directions. Now he knew where to go to get answers, but it was late in tha afternoon. He would have to wait until morning.

≈

It was just after twn in the morning that Josh arrived at the SSPCA headquarters, unexpected and angry. The receptionist made the mistake of saying she didn't know who he was looking for. Josh stared at her with hard eyes as she shrunk away. "Dinnae come it. You must know her. She works for you," he gritted his teeth.

"Have you got an appointment?" the timid, middle-aged woman asked, fumbling with the visitor book on her desk. Josh grabbed the book and spun it around, seized a pen on the desk and scrawled his name like an out of control child, the letters overshooting three lines at a time.

"There. Now can I see her?" Josh did not wait for a reply, he bounded up the narrow staircase to the right of the receptionist's desk, passing the blue-green walls and framed animal prints of cute cats and shaggy dogs, and the poster of a tortured bag of bones that was a pit pony, gawking out in silence from the wall. On a small table was a bust in dark onyx of a horse's head, which shook as Josh bounced past. Then he was through the swinging double-doors at the top of the staircase and into the open plan office filled with computer terminals and four-sided desks, each with swivel chairs in attendance and shirt-wearing staff tapping away on keyboards – at least they were tapping away until the doors crashed against the wall in dramatic fashion and Josh entered.

He let his eyes skip across the upturned faces staring his way. He saw Katrina immediately and headed towards her.

"Surprised to see me?" His voice trembled with anger. Two men jumped into his path, he pushed one aside with ease. The other grappled his left arm and refused to let go. Josh tried to shake him off while throwing glances to Katrina, who stood at her desk with her hands resting on the back of her chair. "Where have you taken her?" Josh called.

Another man joined the fray, and then two security men emerged from a door at the far side of the office.

"Josh, it was for its own good, and yours," said Katrina.

"My ain good!" Josh struggled to free himself from the two men holding him back and felt himself being dragged towards the floor. "Listen to me, Katrina. Get this lot aff me before I gie them the heid." The air was being squeezed from his body by the tightening crush as the two men, now joined by two others, pinned him to the floor. Josh's right arm was twisted behind his back. "I've come to talk, get them aff me."

Katrina stood mute and frozen as Josh struggled under the heaving mass of bodies, and then he too stopped struggling. In a suspended moment no one spoke, the men holding Josh down were suddenly unsure what to do next, they looked up and waited.

"You can't do this" Katrina broke the silence.

"Whit. I cannae save a dolphin?" Josh blurted out, his lungs short of air beneath the weight of his captors as he struggled to lift his head from the floor.

"Josh…"

"Dae yi think I'm mad. Is that it?" Josh pulled at his right arm, but his bid for freedom failed. "You've got to get that dolphin back into the sea by the full moon. You've got to do it, Katrina. Listen to me." He saw her shake her head, averting her eyes from him and looking into the mid-distance. He was pulled to his feet by four of the men who had held him down. His arms were held tightly behind his back. Facing Katrina, he spluttered, "Remember Cramond."

A tear started to fill the corner of Katrina's left eye as the childhood memory of that day on the beach returned. A dusty nerve was struck and it short-circuited her thoughts. She waved a hand at the men who were restraining Josh. "It's okay, let him go."

"Are you sure, Miss?" one of the men questioned in disbelief, looking nervously at his colleagues.

Katrina nodded. "Yes. Let him go. I know him."

The men released their grip. Josh looked a mess in his now disheveled clothes. Katrina walked up and stared into his eyes, testing his sincerity. "Come with me," she said and led him in silence back out of the office, down the stairs and past the reception, then out into the car park at the back of the building. The office windows overlooked the car park. Katrina and Josh were aware of faces pressed against the glass panes on the second floor, observing them. Katrina stood directly in front of Josh.

"So we're back to Cramond," she said.

"Aye."

"Are you trying to send another piece of my childhood down the pan?"

"Whit?" Josh's anger mounted. "No, you're no understanding. I'm telling you the truth. Dae yi think I'd dredge up a thing like this and then lie?"

"Why not?" Katrina responded. "Josh, you can't expect me to go along with your story that you've diagnosed a sick dolphin and you know what is best for it. There are experts who have been trained in rescuing and looking after these creatures. You shouldn't have taken it from the beach in the first place."

"Katrina, if that dolphin disnae get back in the sea in three days' time it's gonna die anyway."

A starling started chirping on a fence as a seagull hovered for a moment observing the scene before continuing its roof top patrol.

"How can you be so sure?" Katrina asked.

"I know. Dinnae ask me to explain. I just know and I wouldnae have come here if it wasn't important. So are you going to help me?"

Another silence.

"I can't," Katrina's head dropped and her eyes no longer engaged his.

"Whit do you mean you can't?" Josh waved his arms in wild circles.

"The dolphin isn't in our custody anymore. It's being looked after by professionals."

Josh slapped the palm of his hand against his forehead. "Where?"

"I can't tell you."

"Hey, I thought we were friends." He pulled back and looked at her long and hard, he raised a hand to his face and felt the day-old stubble around his chin.

"There's only so much I can help you with. If you're as smart as you're trying to tell me you are about dolphins then you'll work it out," said Katrina.

The chirping starling on the fence became silent and then took flight across the car park.

"I thought I knew you," the anger had gone from Josh's voice.

Katrina dropped her gaze and focused on the gravel at their feet. "I thought I knew you too." She walked past him, back towards the office building. Josh stood silent, watching her go and expecting her to turn around and give him a sign, an indication, to toss him a scrap of friendship back. But the smoked glass door closed behind Katrina and she was gone.

So that was that. A golden childhood friendship, which had sustained his heart in the loneliest of times, has been shattered. Josh felt something had been ripped from his insides. A grieving pain seized him as he journeyed home, engulfed in a shroud of sorrow that blocked out the world. He did not realise he was home until he heard the door slam shut as his back slumped against it. He stood for a moment facing the brooding hush of the empty house and called out Suzy's name. There was no response. Then he called out for Dolly. Again, there was only silence. Finally, and much quieter, he called Katrina's name. He listened to the echo of his voice diminish into nothing.

"No, and why would anyone have been here," he cursed under his breath. With the walking gait of a defeated man he managed the few steps to reach the settee in the living room, where he sat and contemplated all that had unfolded. It was Katrina who loomed largest in his thoughts. The sweetheart of his schooldays, they had shared a seemingly unbreakable bond of friendship. His heart raced faster in her company. He had been enthralled and captivated by her beauty and gentle mannerisms, by her grounded, pragmatic logic and her empathy and sense of natural justice. How he'd missed those qualities in the years and decades that had passed since their dalliances of youth.

A spinning wheel of blades was churning and shredding his emotions. He felt betrayed by someone for whom betrayal was an alien concept, or so he had thought. She had offered him nothing, not even a crumb of hope.

For hours he sat. In his mind he replayed the painful events of the day. Katrina's final words resonated, though he wasn't sure why. "You'll work it out," she had said. Her words were stuck on loop-play in his head. Was there some unspoken cue he was missing?

It was six in the evening and he had been sitting in the living room of the empty house watching the growing shadows as he waited for the moment that he could once more go to The Gannet. But there was to be no Gannet time this evening. As the mock-Georgian mantelpiece clock struck six, the dust from the day's confrontation settled and he saw his next move.

"The aquarium." Jumping from the leather settee he grabbed the phone directory lying in the corner of the room and flicked through its pages until he found the entry he was looking for and read the address.

Of course, the aquarium was shut by the time he bounded up its granite steps a little after seven-thirty in the evening. The last stragglers were heading home from their office jobs, with the top button on their shirts undone, ties crooked, and briefcases weighing down their lives as they filed along the pavements to Waverley train station and the taxi ranks. Their eyes were downcast deliberately to avoid meeting those of strangers. There was a moment's excitement as a match burst into flower, the red glow of a cigarette its legacy. Josh watched them all; each a lost soul heading into the night to distant, warm homes and the surety of repeating the whole mind-numbing exercise tomorrow and the next day and the next forty years. The procession entranced him as he paced along the top step outside the city aquarium, quietly considering his next move.

The building was shut and would not reopen until the morning. There was still plenty of time to get back to The Gannet and make the best of the night. Maybe a belly full of piss would make things clear.

Such theories did not take long to seed in his mind and he was about to step away when he saw a scrap of paper skipping past the door and skirting around the edge of the silent building. The paper had the colour of a ten-pound note, but it was moving too quickly on the cold, northern breeze to see clearly. Payment for the bus rides to town and back would be justice indeed. The chase led him into the twilight darkness at the side of the aquarium building where plumes of steam rose from silver flumes amid an array of poky windows, some cracked, others unwashed since time immemorial. Here was the lost home of crisp bags and chip papers, blown into the neglected shrubbery fringing the stained and grubby walls.

Josh retrieved the scrap of paper and held it up to the dim light emanating from one of the small, rectangular windows of the building. His quarry turned out to be nothing more than a faded sweet wrapper.

He threw it back on the ground. As he turned to return to the front of the building there was a sudden expulsion of steam from one of the flumes at the side of the building. It attracted his attention upwards to a small window, which he noticed had been left open a tiny crack.

There was always a way in for Josh when there was an open window, and the ten-foot climb up a bricked-up windowsill was easy, especially as he was sober. He squeezed his left hand into the gap between the open window and the flaking paint of the window frame, as he did the skin on the back of his hand was pulled with the strain but there is enough free movement to wiggle his fingers and feel the window catch move – another inch was all it needed. Biting his tongue to quell a cry of pain he tried again. The catch clicked and the small window swung freely open.

Cat-like, he clambered through the tiny aperture, dropping arms and head first on to a table and straightening himself back up as his eyes adjusted to the semi-light thrown out from the weak illumination of a red emergency exit sign nearby. All was quiet, but there was ambient warmth seeping down the corridor he was now in – it was a moist, tropical warmth emanating from the warm waters of the aquarium tanks housed inside. He had only to follow the source of the warm air to be among them; and this he soon achieved.

The first giant tank was filled with silvery, Mediterranean fish that circled in a large group like a fragmented, living mirror. A mostly white lobster, at least a foot and a half long, skulked inside a cavern of stone and shingle at the bottom of the tank. Josh moved on, passing an open tank of stingrays and eagle rays and what appeared to be prehistoric leftover sand crawlers. In another tank vibrantly coloured striped fish and angelfish in shades of electric blue and sunshine yellow populated a coral reef display. As he walked he was aware of the echo of his own footsteps and he adjusted his gait to quieten the impact of his feet on the floor.

The next room was vast, and it needed to be to accommodate the immense tank that held an underwater shipwreck with half a dozen sharks prowling around it. The lights in the room were turned off, and everything blacked out but for a few tiny underwater tank lights and the green emergency lighting above distant doorways. The cavernous ceiling above reflected a flickering, haunting pall.

He had a nagging feeling that he and the fish were not alone. At first he had thought the occasional noise he heard was the banging of pipes elsewhere in the building, the expanding and contracting of heating ducts, but now he crouched low next to the piranha tank and listened to the steady rhythm of approaching footsteps through the rooms of aquarium tanks. Unhurried footsteps were following his route. To his left, a ten feet dash away, an emergency door light illuminated a possible escape route, but it was too risky now to chance opening the door. The footsteps were near.

A beam of light broke through the darkness and pierced the waters of the piranha tank inches above his crouched body and bowed head. There were voices, two people talking. Now as he listened, Josh could make out the softer patting of a second pair of feet. They had entered the room and a single torch beam scanned the walls. He reduced his breathing to the same shallow, silent gulp of the fish that swam in the tank.

"Probably those pipes again," one of the security men said.

"Yeah, guess so."

The footsteps stopped; there was a slight shuffling. They were looking around. Josh tried to follow the direction of the torchlight but dared not move.

"So what happened to that dolphin they brought in?"

"Took it out again, down south somewhere. Too big for them to keep it in a tank here," the other man replied. Josh's ears perked up. The torchlight vanished and the men started walking away. Crouching as low as possible, Josh skipped across the room, stopping behind each of the tanks until he was at the door from where he had a clear line of vision down the corridor and could see the shadowy silhouettes of the security men vanishing into the distance. The men were still talking about the dolphin. He strained to catch every word he could. They had taken it away to a bigger aquarium, some place down in England, near Scarborough.

"Shit," Josh thumped his fist against his thigh. He had to get out of the aquarium. The window he had climbed through was still open, just as he had left it. Hopping onto the table beneath it he clambered up and squeezed his body back through the tiny aperture. The security men did not hear him and he jumped down into the darkness of the back courtyard and stumbled on an unseen rock as he hit the ground.

It would have been the perfect escape, but for the blue light flashing against the opposite wall. A police car was parked at the steps of the aquarium with its roof light rotating silently. From the corner of the building Josh peered around and saw two police officers at the top of the steps by the main entrance, exactly where he had been pacing less than an hour before. The officers were talking to two security men; Josh assumed they are the same two from inside. It must be coincidence, he told himself. As far as he knew he hadn't alerted them to his presence. He ducked back into the shadows and headed around to the unlit side of the building, past the steaming flumes and the irregular-shaped courtyard that doubled as a service area. A large van was parked there. It must belong to the aquarium, he surmised as he gave it a sideways glance and quickly crossed to the far side of the courtyard where the darkest shadows were to be found.

He jumped back from the corner as he spotted two shapes moving towards him. There was a shout and a rush of running feet. The police officers had seen him. He raced back through the unlit courtyard and reached the van he had passed moments earlier. Grabbing the back door latch, he rolled it open and clambered inside, closing it quickly behind. His heart was racing, but he denied it the oxygen it craved as he held his breath and became a dormant lump on the wooden floor, bathed in the creamy city light filtering through the yellowing Perspex roof panels. The van was empty but for a large glass tank half-filled with water and mounted on a steel frame towards the front end. The still water jumped into agitated ripples as the van shook and the roller back door fizzed open.

"Right you, out!" commanded a voice.

CHAPTER THIRTEEN

HEARTBROKEN

Katrina has been home for more than an hour, but she had not changed out of her work uniform. Even her cap remained on her head. She sat in the armchair that faced the window. Purshaw the cat was stretched out on the windowsill with one eye asleep and the other lazily regarding her. For almost half-an-hour Katrina had cradled a cup of tea in her hands. It had long gone cold, but she had not refreshed it. She had not felt inclined to move from the armchair. Instead, she stared at the dark sky outside the window.

The door to the flat opened and closed. "I'm home," Lisa called out. Katrina was going to reply, but didn't.

"You in there?" Lisa called again from the entrance hall as she hung her coat on a wall peg.

"Yeah," Katrina mustered a muted reply.

Lisa came into the living room and saw her flatmate seated in the armchair, illuminated against the evening darkness by a lamp on the table beside her. She noticed Katrina was still in her SSPCA clothes. "What are you doing still dressed like that. Are you going back to work tonight?" she asked.

"No." Katrina barely turned her head to acknowledge her friend. "I got distracted."

"By what?"

"My thoughts. Things that happened today."

Lisa sat on the armchair next to Katrina and leaned across to gently touch her arm. "What happened?" she asked softly.

"Josh came to the office – angry. Really angry."

"And?"

Katrina lifted her a hand to rub her right hand, then lowered it again to her lap, where she cradled the cold cup of tea.

"I'm not sure if I've done the right thing," she replied.

"With the dolphin?" Lisa said. "Hey, of course you have. It's your job. That's what you do; you look after animals. That dolphin's in much safer hands now than it was in some daftie's bathtub."

Katrina said nothing. It looked as though she had nodded her head, but it was such a weak movement that Lisa could not be sure.

"We both agreed last night what a loser he was. Remember?" Lisa put an arm around Katrina. "Come on, Kat. He was someone special to you when you were younger. But people change, and not always for the better."

Katrina's attention remained fixed on the sliver of night sky she could glimpse outside the window.

"You're better off without him in your life," Lisa said. "The past is the past. You've seen who he is now. Josh the boy is gone. Josh the man is the reality, complete with his faults – his drinking and questionable grasp of social norms."

Lisa stopped for a moment and waited for Katrina's response. But there was none.

"Trust your instincts, Kat," she continued. "You summed him up perfectly last night. Don't doubt yourself now. Whatever he said today, you've got to move on. You've done the right thing. The dolphin's safe."

Lisa watched Katrina intently, but again there was no reaction. She changed tack. "Okay, listen. I don't know about you, but I'm hungry. How about a carry-out supper. You in?"

At last Katrina broke away from her trance. "Sure. That'd be good."

Lisa stood up; when she reached the door she turned. "I'll be back in ten minutes. Put the kettle on and we'll have tea too."

Katrina nodded then listened as the front door of the flat closed. Lisa's footsteps echoed on the concrete stairwell as she headed back to the ground floor. Once the footsteps faded away the flat was silent again.

Mixed emotions and tangled thoughts crowded Katrina's mind. Josh had seemed so sure, so certain about what he knew. There had been something unnerving about his insistence. Katrina returned to her trance as pictures from the past tumbled through her head, reminders of her youthful years and the times together with Josh; the unbreakable bond they had shared. It meant something. Was she now to believe that the boy who helped save the baby dolphin was really so different from the man he had become?

She caught herself and shook her head. No, the years had changed him, as they had changed her. She'd acted with integrity. She had stepped in to prevent harm to the animal. It was her duty. She was in the right. Lisa's pragmatic assessment of it all made perfect sense. And yet, there had been something in Josh's eyes that had resonated in her thoughts and cast doubt on her assumptions.

She was sure she had done the right thing, yet at the same time she wasn't.

The front door opened. Lisa was back and was laden down with a warm bag of carry-out food. "Is the tea ready?" she called out.

Katrina jumped up from the armchair. "Sorry. I'll put the kettle on."

CHAPTER FOURTEEN

DRINKING TALK

Josh was in a van, but it wasn't the one he'd tried to hide in at the aquarium. It jumped as it hit a pothole in the road. From a tiny window a little above his eyeline he could see the roofs and upper floors of offices. It was central Edinburgh and the sky was almost blanketed with cloud.

There was no feeling of heat or comfort in the confines of the cubicle where he now found himself. The transporter van carried ten prisoners, although he had only seen four of them as they were led to the van from the police station cells where they had spent the previous night. The cubicle was just large enough for Josh to stand up in and turn around. A small bench against the wall acted as a seat. The locked door faced out on the other side to a narrow central corridor. There were five identical cubicles on the opposite side.

Josh slumped on the bench seat, its hard plastic jarring the bones of his pelvis. He held his head in his hands and stared at the floor and his worn shoes. Soon the van would be outside the sheriff's court and he would have to atone for his actions. The duty solicitor at the police station had spent over an hour going through Josh's story about the carpet and what he was doing at the aquarium. Katrina had not made any complaint about his behaviour at the SSPCA office, but the solicitor had received word that others at the office had noted that he'd turned up the previous day enquiring about the dolphin and had then been caught at the aquarium in the evening. The solicitor told him this extra background information would undoubtedly be used against him to explain what he was doing at the aquarium building.

Of course there was no proof that he had been inside the aquarium. The officers had only caught him hiding in the back of the van in the courtyard – that wasn't much of a rap. But having the dolphin in his bathroom in the first place, well, that was a different kettle of fish.

The van hit another pothole, throwing Josh into the air a few inches so that his backside slammed against the plastic bench again. He winced and stood up, steadying himself against the tight walls that brushed his shoulders as the van lurched along the uneven road. The buildings outside the spy hole window were much taller now and had squared off facades of imposing grandeur. The city centre had been reached. He felt the van slowing and turn a tight corner to the left and then another to the right before it came to a halt. Then the van started moving again, this time reversing into position. It had arrived at the court building.

A security guard opened the door to the cubicle and beckoned Josh out. For a guard he was short – short, but meaty – with muscle bulking out his forearms and layers of fat around his tubby stomach, which overhung the belt on his trousers. A stainless steel key chain hung from the belt in a loop stretching to a few inches below the guard's knees. The sleeves of his white shirt were rolled up to his elbows, and there was the blue logo of an eagle and the letter 'S' emblazoned on his left breast pocket. His eyes were hidden behind a pair of smoked sunglasses.

"Time to go," the guard said, the thin line of his lips barely moving as he spoke and gestured for Josh to vacate the cubicle. Josh responded, stepping forward. The guard produced a set of handcuffs from his trouser pocket and snapped one half around Josh's left wrist with the other around his right. There was a tricky manoeuvre out of the cubicle and along the narrow corridor in the centre of the van, which had to be negotiated sideways.

Outside, and despite the grey, overcast clouds, Josh felt the obscured sun's warmth as his eyes adjusted to the brightness of the day. A flock of pigeons circled the roof tops, scanning the streets for easy pickings or bread being thrown by tourists – a habit Josh had never understood; why feed those dumbo creatures that didn't even have the sense to move out of the way when you were about to tread on them? Today the birds were in their proper place. Everything was in its proper place. He was the only thing that wasn't in its proper place.

The back entrance to the sheriff's court was hardly the most picturesque sight in Edinburgh, adorned as it was with a smelly industrial waste bin and a layout which could have been designed with building blocks by a three-year-old kid who had never seen a straight line before. That's what Josh told himself as he looked around. Not that he was complaining. His lips were tightly clamped as the guard led him towards the side door of the building, beyond lay the holding cells beneath the main courtroom. The unforgiving building had already swallowed a prisoner.

Then there was a noise, a shout of something incoherent and unfriendly. Josh turned around to see what it was. One of his arms was practically wrenched from its socket as the guard looked back at the van from where a commotion inside began to spill outside. Another guard fell backwards down the retractable steps and landed on his arse, his arms sprawling on the ground as he dropped his handcuffs. A skinhead youth popped his head out of the van and stared at the guard on the ground. The youth looked up at Josh and his captor. There was the briefest flash of a two-fingered salute and then the youth bounded from the van, his Doc Martin boots clumping either side of the felled guard as he dashed away.

"Get the bugger, Ewan," the guard holding Josh shouted at his downed colleague as he dragged Josh back towards the van and snapped the handcuff off his wrist and onto the handle of the van door.

"You stay here," the guard ordered as he ran after the fleeing skinhead, who was already being pursued by the first of the security men, who had picked his sorry arse off the ground.

Sometimes luck had a strange way of finding Josh when he least expected it or had given up all hope of ever seeing it. It was a surreal moment as he rattled the handcuff holding him to the van door handle and noticed the loose screw on the handle a few centimetres shy of flush. It was enough for his free right hand to grasp and begin turning, applying pressure to the tiny screwhead as it emerged from the side panel. The guards and the skinhead had vanished from view. Josh turned the screw faster. It popped out and fell at his feet. With a yank of his free hand he twisted the door handle out of shape, opening a gap at the bottom to allow the handcuff to slip free. But as he did so a third guard re-emerged from the back door of the sheriff's courthouse where he had earlier deposited a prisoner. The guard marched up to Josh, who now held his handcuffed hand against the bent door handle, praying it appeared to be secured in place.

"Whit's happening?" the big guard demanded. He was tall, almost as tall as the prison van.

"Some skinheed broke loose, did a runner. Your pals chased him doon the street," Josh replied.

"Where?"

Josh gestured with his head and the guard marched away, quickly breaking into a trot.

"See you later, sucker," Josh whispered as he took his hand away from the van door handle and shoved it into his trouser pocket, the loose handcuff dangling against his thigh. Then he was off, taking it easy and coolly so as not to attract attention to himself. However, the casual stroll soon turned into a more frantic hop and skip as he felt a flush of prickly heat and nerves wash over him the further he got from the van. There was no going back now. He was almost out of sight. The streets rolled back like a magic carpet as he sauntered along, then he picked up the pace until, a few corners away and assured that he was not being tailed, he broke into a proper jog, one hand dangling the loose handcuff that he tried unsuccessfully to grasp out of view as he bounded along.

He knew the road back from the city centre and stuck more or less to the bus route, cursing his lack of money each time he was passed by a rattling, claret-coloured number 17 or number 19 bus. His feet were warm to the point of sweating by the time he reached the brow of the hill from where the housing scheme spread out before him, a sight that would signal despair to an outsider, but to a long-term resident was a welcoming view. Two hours of hard walking from the town centre and he had a raging thirst.

The door of The Gannett opened and Josh walked in.

"Och aye, look who it isnae," greeted Tam Tam from behind the bar. Josh squinted his eyes as they adjusted to the perma-gloom of the pub interior. There was a reasonable crowd for a mid-afternoon session.

"I've nae money. Can yi put me on the slate?" he asked.

Tam Tam nodded and produced a pint of heavy. Josh pulled his left hand from his pocket and reached for the pint of heavy. The handcuffs still attached to his wrist hit the bar top.

"Nice bracelet," said Tam Tam.

"The best – this isnae imitation; it's real pig issue."

Tam Tam nodded.

"But they'll no get me that easy, ken what 'am saying?" Josh continued.

Tam Tam nodded some more. The story of Josh's arrest had done a few circuits of the pub already – gossip never took long to reach The Gannet. In fact, most gossip in the neighbourhood was born between the crooked tables and fag-burnt wooden floor, steeped as it was in stale beer spilt over the decades. But Josh's escape was another matter. By the time the usual suspects of the evening crew had assembled Josh had retold the story, refined it and boiled it down to a well-crafted patter with which to regale all. Angus, Stovey and Blind

Peter listened without saying a word. Peter could hear the occasional jingling of the handcuffs – that was the proof – and Stovey had not raised any objections to the tale.

"Will they no come looking fur yi once they realise you've given them the slip?" Stovey asked as he bought a fourth pint for skint Josh.

"Aye, sure they will. But that's no ma main concern at the mo. I'll jist keep a low profile for the next day or two until I dae what I have to dae."

"What's that then?" Big Angus cradled his pint in one of his huge hands, his fingers completely hiding the glass as he cushioned it against his stomach.

"Rescue a dolphin."

Stovey spat a mouthful of beer back into his pint glass – a first.

Tam Tam noticed. "Summit wrang wi the beer?" he inquired, rubbing his hands dry on a bar towel as he approached from the other side of the counter. Tam Tam had been too far away to overhear the conversation. Stovey filled him in.

"No, but there's summit wrang wi Josh. He's going tae rescue a dalfin."

Josh waited for Stovey's sniggering to subside. There had been no reaction from Peter and Angus, although Angus stroked a hand through his beard thoughtfully.

"Where is it?" Tam Tam asked.

"England."

"England!" Stovey chortled.

"And I need some help," Josh added.

"Too right yi fucking do."

"Zip it, Stovey," Angus spoke up in his deep voice. His words took Josh by surprise to say nothing of Stovey who glanced twice at Angus to see if the big man was jesting. The interruption allowed Josh to expand on his plan to head to Scarborough and liberate the dolphin from its captivity in an aquarium and return it to the Firth of Forth where it could reunite with its family group. Angus listened intently.

Stovey, still smarting from his surprise chastising, said nothing. Peter grunted as he supped his pint and stretched his string vest.

"How are you going tae achieve all this in two days?" Tam Tam asked as he poured another two pints for Josh and Stovey.

"I've already seen the van that'll be able to carry the dolphin back. It's got a waater tank and everything."

"How dae yi know all this?" Stovey piped up as he grabbed his refreshed pint. "How dae yi ken this dalfin needs to go back in the water. Who told yi?"

"I've got a friend who knows all aboot them. This is my mission and I'm going to dae it with or without your help." Josh sucked on the forthy head of his pint of heavy as he waited for his words to sink in.

"Whit kind o' help are yi expecting?" Angus asked, his hidden pint still cradled against his stomach. He was slipping back in the evening's drinking stakes, but no one was likely to make an issue of it now that he had already dished a yellow card warning to Stovey for his lip.

"I need help driving the van for a start. It's going tae be a non-stop roond trip there and back, driving in shifts."

Angus nodded.

"Then there's the little matter of getting the dolphin oot of the aquarium and into the van and getting her back into the sea."

Stovey was counting an imaginary number on his fingers. He stopped and looked Josh in the eye. "So whit's in it for you and everyone else?"

"The dolphin goes back where she belongs."

"And?" Stovey awaited the rider.

"That's it. End of story."

"Hang on. You're prepared to nick a van, drive two hundred miles, nick a dalfin and then drive back and let it go....for nowt?"

Josh nodded.

"Noble," Blind Peter joined the conversation, leaning against the bar in his pants and vest and staring unsighted at the corner of the bar where the wall met the ceiling.

"Bampot, if you ask me," Stovey rolled his eyes. "Have yi no had enough o' getting nicked. Whit if the cops catch yi?"

"I'll no get caught. I've got away from them the noo, aye?"

"Dinnae speak too soon. There's a jam sandwich pulled up outside," warned Tam Tam, straining his neck to see above the half-frosted panes of the pub windows and outside where a police patrol car had driven up and parked.

"Fuck," Josh slammed down his pint and nervously flicked his head to look from one side to the other.

"In the corner wi yi," Peter's voice was calm and measured.

"Whit?" Josh was incredulous at the blind man's suggestion.

"Dinnae argue. In the corner behind the table and the rest o' us will pile you up with coats." Peter was already walking across to the table he couldn't see, but which he knew was there as it had been every day since he first started drinking at The Gannet twenty years ago. "The rest o' you lads get your jackets off and throw them on top of him, then sit roond the table."

"You're no taking anything more aff are yi?" Josh asked as he followed the barely dressed Peter. When Josh reached the wooden bench behind the corner table he crawled underneath it. Angus was the first to throw his heavy work jacket on top of Josh, then there was another thud as two more jackets followed simultaneously.

Beneath the jackets Josh could hear only the muffled voices of Angus and Stovey as they crowded around the table. It quickly became warm beneath the overcoats and he wanted to scratch an itch on the side of his arm, but he dared not move as an image flashed across his mind's eye of the police officers entering the bar and looking around.

The muffled voices continued for what seemed an eternity. Surely the police had gone by now. Had the others forgotten he was still buried, roasting beneath the coats? Josh wondered. His breathing became shallower and sweat formed across his forehead. The discomfort was now becoming unbearable and the hardness of the bench that pressed against his side, arms and leg was excruciating.

"All right under there?" Stovey asked, finally pulling the coats clear and letting the ale-impregnated cool air of the bar rush across Josh's senses once again. Josh blinked rapidly as his eyes readjusted to the light.

"How long was I under there?"

"Aboot an hour."

"Whit! Did they hang aboot that long?"

"Nah, they cleared off after five minutes, but we thought you looked so snug and peaceful under there that we didnae want to disturb yi."

"Bastard!" Josh threw the rest of the jackets off as he sat up at the table. Peter had blindly wandered to the bar to refresh his pint.

"So, are yi going to help me?" Josh asked again.

"What kind of help dae yi need?" Angus held in a belch, but it reverberated in his throat like the sound of a seal. Stovey had stopped his sniggering. Josh waited until Peter had shuffled back to the table with his pint, his unerring sense of direction bringing him safely across the room without the need for eyes.

"I need help wi the van – driving it and carrying the dolphin." Josh looked at the faces of his three friends. There was no visible reaction from Angus or Peter. Stovey was shaking his head from side to side, his eyes lowered so not to meet Josh's.

"Well, if I can't get any help I'll dae it myself," Josh concluded.

"We'd be accessories to a crime," Stovey stated the obvious, guessing that Peter and Angus had not yet considered the fact.

"Aye, we would," Angus nodded, "but only if we got caught." A thin smile crossed the big man's face. Josh noticed.

At what point in the evening's proceedings agreement was reached that the three would offer Josh their assistance was not altogether clear. But a pact evolved verbally and the four left with instructions to meet at the city aquarium the following evening as darkness fell.

Leaving The Gannet, Josh headed back home, staggering a little, catching himself on the side of garden walls and hedges as he had so many times before on his homeward-bound trek from the pub. As he reached the house he fumbled in his pocket for his keys and realised they had been taken from him at the police station. He cursed as he slumped against the wooden gate and looked up at the silent night sky. There wasn't another soul in the street so late at night. He fumbled in his pockets again, just in case his addled mind has got it wrong and the keys were actually there. They weren't. His head dropped, then he looked up at his darkened home and realised it wasn't totally in darkness.

He blinked in an exaggerated manner. There was the glow of a dim light from inside the house. Through the frosted glass of the front door he could see a light from within; it appeared to be from the kitchen at the back. He pushed himself off the wooden gate with the force of his buttock muscles alone and staggered towards the door, banging the glass with the flat of his right palm and then leaving it stuck against the pane to support himself as he awaited a reply from whoever was inside. There was no response, so he repeated his three slaps against the glass, only harder this time.

"Suzy? Is that you in there? Let me in, hen. I've no got ma keys." He bent down and opened the flap of the letterbox and repeated himself, his eyes trying to focus on the distant light from the kitchen and whoever might be inside.

"The cops have been roond here looking for you," Suzy shouted in response from the kitchen.

"No shit!"

"What's that?" Suzy called out.

"I said, is that so," Josh replied through the letterbox. "Come on Suzy, I dinnae want to stand oot here all night shouting through a letterbox. Let me in, eh"

"Well that's too bad, because you're no coming in all pissed up." And Suzy meant it. The light of the kitchen went out and the landing light went on. Through the letterbox Josh saw Suzy shimmy past and go up the stairs. His calls were not returned. The hall landing light went out and the house was in darkness. For another 10 minutes he called through the letterbox, pleading to be let in, but there was no response. Tired, he gave up and slumped to a seated position with his back against the door, knees up to his chin and fell asleep.

The dark hours moved on and daybreak came in its muted way to the housing scheme. Josh slept on, oblivious to the dawn chorus of birds resting on the roofs and telephone wires. Then his world collapsed – or rather the front door that had supported his back all night opened and he fell backwards, his head hitting the hall floor with a thud. His startled eyes opened and he saw Suzy standing over him.

"Does this mean I can come in?" he asked, groggily getting to his feet.

"Look at the state of you," Suzy did not hide her contempt.

"I'd look perfectly normal if I didn't just have to sleep on the pavement all night."

"Sure I don't need to check your pockets this time, in case you're bringing in another dolphin?" Suzy crossed her arms.

"No, you don't."

"Or how about a blonde-haired hussy? No got a fancy woman with you this time?"

"You dinnae understand," Josh replied as he stepped past her into the house.

"Well that's the first sensible thing you've said for a while. Too right I don't understand. Care to enlighten me?"

Josh shook his head. "Later."

"Aye, later," Suzy watched as Josh vanished into the front room. She heard him flop onto the leather couch. At the same time her mobile phone rang and she answered it. "Hiya Maxine. Yeah, guess what the cat dragged in. Aye."

Josh could half hear the phone conversation, but the urge to sleep was overwhelming and he drifted away, fully clothed, on the settee. He slept for the remainder of the daylight hours and awoke as the broom of dusk was sweeping away all but the smallest reminders of the day now gone. He stared at his watch, then realising how little time there was to get to the rendezvous with the others he jumped from the couch. If Suzy was in the house he did not notice. He couldn't see any lights on or hear any movement, but his primary concern was getting out of the house, which he did with a fumbling dash.

Upstairs, in the semi-darkness of the bedroom, Suzy was dozing when she heard the front door slam. She jumped from her slumber to watch from the window the silhouette of Josh jogging away down the pavement, a fleeting ghost between the skirts of orange illumination cast by the streetlights. Her mobile phone flicked open emitting a dazzling whiteness to the dark room.

"Maxine. Okay, he just left, aye. Can you see him? Right, I'll be at the door in a minute, pull up at the gate," Suzy closed the phone and replaced it in the front pocket of her jeans as she turned to leave the room.

Josh thought he would be the first to arrive but he found Angus already sitting on the granite steps in front of the aquarium building staring down at the manicured lawns and gardens as the thinnest glow of twilight after-burn panned across the rooftops and through the branches of the trees, which swayed in the breeze.

It would be completely dark by eight. There was about an hour to go. Josh had hoped to be first on the scene so that he could have time to gather his thoughts and steel himself for the job ahead. When he saw Angus he was tempted to keep walking, averting his gaze until he was out of sight and then hang back around the corner until nearer the time so that he could figure things out. Perhaps that was the wisest move. Two men together outside the closed aquarium could draw suspicion. Who knew if there were any closed-circuit television cameras trained on the front of the building? There must be cameras somewhere.

But Josh's concerns were not strong enough to override his sense of friendship, which compelled him to climb the steps and join his big friend. After all, he had half expected to find that it was only the beer that had been talking in The Gannet the night before. But he had been proven wrong, at least on one count, for Angus showed he was as good as his word.

"All right?" Josh greeted as he approached. Angus was startled for a moment. He had been admiring the dappled colours of the flowers in the public gardens; his daydream broken he turned to see Josh standing over him.

"Fine, I finished early. Thought I'd come straight here and no get side-tracked back at The Gannet," Angus said.

"Aye, it's that time," Josh checked his watch, even though he had glanced at it four times within the last two minutes. On a normal day he would expect to find Angus, Stovey and Blind Peter in the pub by now starting their evening session. It was hard to imagine that Stovey would not be doing so. He joined Angus on the top step and looked across the gardens, trying hard to think of something to say but unable to come up with anything compelling to share, so they sat in silence.

It was as the light of day faded to a deep purple, etched against the western horizon above the rooftops and chimney pots, that a figure appeared slowly shuffling beneath the streetlights. The gait of the man's walk alerted Josh that Peter has arrived and, as ever, was dressed only in his pants and vest and worn-out brown shoes. His white stick was thrust out ahead of him at an angle, sweeping a semi-circle back and forth as he checked for obstacles. Josh got up and met him at the bottom of the steps leading to the aquarium, taking hold of his elbow and guiding him to where Angus sat.

"Just Stovey then," Josh announced when the three were together.

Angus remained seated but looked up at Peter and Josh. "Do you think he'll come?"

"He said he would." Josh flicked his wrist to see his watch. There was still ten minutes before eight o'clock. They hadn't specified an exact time, but it was now dark and eight o'clock seemed like a good cut-off point. They waited. By quarter past the hour there was still no sign of the fourth man.

"Right, let's go."

"Stovey's not coming then?" Angus observed as he stood.

"Disnae look like it," Josh answered as he pulled Peter up to his feet. The hushed group made their way around to the side of the building and into the shadows, passing the vapour-expelling flumes. The small torch Josh had brought cast a tiny pool of light on the ground, barely enough to pick out the discarded cans and beer bottles which littered the way. More than once Peter's clicking walking stick picked out a chime as it struck some unseen trash. The van that Josh had jumped into a few nights previous was parked in the same spot. Josh gave a sigh of relief as his torchlight swept along its side.

"I'll take care of the lock and we're off," he said, scurrying across the remainder of the courtyard to the driver's side door of the van. He could hear Angus following and Peter behind, his stick skimming the ground like a metronome.

Switching off his torch, Josh pulled from his jacket pocket a long piece of heavy-duty plastic binding cord and reached up to slide it down between the van window and the inside of the door, feeding it downwards. Eventually it snagged on something and he pulled it back up a few inches and then pushed it back down. "Almost there," he reassured the others as he pulled the binding band up at a slightly different angle. Somewhere within the inner workings of the door it struck the lock mechanism. He smiled as he heard the sweet sound of the catch being unleashed.

"We're in," he announced with glee and pulled open the driver's door. Then his heart skipped a beat and he jumped back, his heart kicked into action again at double speed. There was a dark silhouette sitting in darkness in the driver's seat.

"What kept you?"

Josh recognised the voice and outline of the face. "Stovey?"

"Been waiting about half-an-hour. This is the van you were on about?"

"Aye," Josh gathered his composure.

"Sure aboot that?"

"Aye."

"Well, I thought you said we were going to be inconspicuous."

"We are."

"Well, dae you no think that thing on the side is going to give us away to the first patrol car that sees us?"

Josh stepped back and flicked the torchlight against the side of the panel van. 'Come and meet Sammy the Seal at the City Aquarium' it read in big letters – worse, the entire side of the van was given over to a giant mural of a seal balancing a beach ball on its nose.

CHAPTER FIFTEEN

SCARBOROUGH

"No sign of her," Maxine leaned forward against the car steering wheel to peer through the windscreen as she tailed the van that had exited from the back of the city aquarium building.

Suzy had her eyes trained on the back of the vehicle. "That's got to be them in the van, they've stolen it," she concluded.

"What do they want a van for?"

"That bunch of losers? Who knows?"

The van weaved slightly from side to side as it cantered down the main road heading out of Edinburgh city centre. Following at a distance of 100 metres was the rusty blue car driven by Maxine with Suzy as front seat passenger.

"Still. I didn't see that woman. And you said he didn't mention her earlier?" said Maxine.

Suzy nodded, her eyes focused straight ahead. "Maybe that's where they'll lead us. Something's going on. And why take a van from the aquarium – is he going to catch another dolphin?"

The car lurched sharply to the right as it swung around a tight corner, barely managing to stay within sight of the van as it sped through the city streets.

"Do you think he's worth all this?" Maxine stole a quick sideways glance at her friend.

"I don't know what I think anymore. But I'm not going to let him – or her – make a mockery out of me."

"And what about that animal cruelty woman?" Maxine turned a tight left-hand bend.

"Old flame. It's over between them. She's disgusted at his behaviour; trying to keep a dolphin in the bathroom."

Maxine shook her head. "Then just let him go and dig his own...."

"No. I still....." Suzy fell silent.

"Still, what?"

"He's a waster, but there's something deeper."

"You can't give up on him?"

"He's hurt me Max, he's hurt me real bad – more than anyone. I don't know why he is doing this, why he feels the need for this other...." Suzy couldn't bring herself to say the word.

"He's cheating on you Suzy. No two ways about it."

Suzy sat in silence in the darkness of the car, only the light from the illuminated dashboard and the occasional flash of headlights from a passing car picked out the soft tears that rolled slowly across her cheeks. She turned her head at an angle away from Maxine to hide her distress. "We'll see," she whispered in reply.

Up ahead the van rocked and banked hard as Josh flicked it around a bend and onto the slip road of a dual carriageway. The rain had started to fall almost as soon as they had left the outskirts of Edinburgh. They were less than 20 miles into the journey and already it felt as though time was running out.

"Slow down, they're not after us yet. Drive like this and we'll be pulled over straight away," Stovey pleaded. He was squashed in the middle of the bench seat with Angus and Peter either side like bookends propping him up. The only one of the four with any room was Josh, but even he had to fight for space to grab the gear stick as he drove.

"We want to be there by dawn. In fact, we want to be there well before sun up so we can load up and get oot of sight before someone clocks us," Josh replied.

"Well, you picked the van with the fucking seal on the side. Could yi no just have hired a plain white one or summit?"

"We need the tank in the back of this one," Josh grunted and hoped Stovey was not going to nag all the way to Scarborough.

"When do you think they'll notice it's gone?" Angus pondered.

"No until the morning when they go back to work. By that time we'll have the dolphin and be ready to come back hame," Josh answered.

"Aye, sure, if we've no been nicked beforehand. What speed are you daein?" Stovey added.

The windscreen wipers blurred the falling rain into oily streaks, sparkling with the reflected light of cat's eyes staring up from the road's black tarmac. The centre line cat's eyes were the only external hint of the van's speed as they flashed past against the darkness of the night.

On the dashboard the speedometer needle bounced around close to the 80 miles per hour mark, nippy for such a large van, but Josh ignored Stovey's comment about speeding and stared at the distant red taillights of cars ahead. His foot was hard to the floor, but still the van was the slowest moving vehicle on the road.

And the rain continued to fall.

Josh's thoughts raced ahead, projecting into the future when they would reach Scarborough in the dead of night and follow the street signs to the aquarium. That at least would be easy to find, he convinced himself. Then there was the question of how to get inside. There would surely be a security presence. Perhaps bluffing that it was an official movement of the dolphin would do the trick. The early morning security wouldn't know any different and probably wouldn't care so long as it didn't interrupt their napping time too much.

But would Dolly know who he was? Could she tell he had not abandoned her? What would she say? Had she been cured of the virus? Katrina seemed to think it was an easy remedy.

"Shit," Josh jumped out of his seat as he felt the wheels bumping along the cat's eyes on the verge of the hard shoulder. He pulled at the steering wheel until the van was back in the centre of the carriageway lane.

"Concentrate," Angus' measured voice was stern.

"Aye, we're no good to that dalfin if we end up in a ditch at Berwick," Stovey added unnecessarily. Peter snored, a quiet breathy-type snore. At least someone was not worried about the quality of the driving, Josh thought amusingly.

"Are you going to drive all the way?" Stovey asked.

"Nah. I'm going to walk for ten miles in the middle if that's okay with you – of course I'm going to fucking drive all the way," Josh's tiredness was manifesting as sarcasm.

"I meant are you going to let one of us do some driving…and I'm no including Peter in that equation."

"Ken the way dae yi?"

"A ken the way to Scarborough, just fallow the signs like your daein," Stovey fired back.

Josh had never been south of the border before. He was surprised by how normal things looked. The road signs were the same colour, there were houses and streets as mundane as any in Scotland. The people, the few he had seen through the rain, were huddled beneath umbrellas or with upturned coat collars as they waited by the roadside to cross. The myth of the 'auld enemy' had played tricks on his mind. He had expected something different, more exotic, more ludicrous, more of a target on which to pin the prejudices he had stored up. But the reality was a 'much of a muchness' bland palette that left nothing outstanding to be mocked. Perhaps daylight would cast a different complexion on matters.

The night wore on and it was past three in the morning when they entered the sleeping streets of Scarborough. The rain had stopped, but the roads and pavements glistened with water and there was a cold wind blowing in from the North Sea. Even with the windows shut the piercing, bitter wind could be felt and observed ripping through the railings along the seafront where bare flagpoles rattled as though possessed by the spirits of the bleak sea.

"Now where?" Stovey rubbed his eyes. He had been asleep for much of the journey. The engine was switched off and Josh leaned forward in his seat, staring at the deserted road ahead as it swept around the bay. On one side was the promenade and on the other a high, banked Victorian terrace interspersed with bed and breakfast vacancy notices. Most of the house lights were off, and the sodium streetlights cast a pall of despondency. Josh ventured out into the biting cold, slamming the van door shut behind him and thrusting his hands deep into his trouser pockets as he stood facing the dark sea, tasting the salty essence whipped into the night air by the wailing wind.

"So where is it?" Stovey asked as he zipped up his coat, standing behind Josh's right shoulder.

Josh had not heard him leave the van, but he did not react to the sudden company. "We'll find it. It's no gonna be hidden," he answered.

"Aye, well let's get going. I want to be in and oot and back hame to ma own bed before morning."

Angus arrived a moment later. He had walked to the road junction just behind the van. There was a sign for the aquarium pointing to the left, he informed the other two. The streets of the English seaside town were deathly quiet, as was to be expected in the middle of the night on a weekday. There was no sign of life anywhere. The freezing conditions only added to the sense of desolation. Angus had seen no one during his short walk back from the road sign, but if he had lifted his head a little higher against the northeasterly wind he might have noticed the rusty blue car parked further along the road, and the two women sitting in darkness and ducking low to the dashboard – watching. Suzy and Maxine regained their seating positions as Angus retreated and re-grouped with Josh and Stovey before all three quickly reboarded the van. Josh turned the van around and took the road he had sailed past moments earlier. The engine of the parked car fired up and it too moved off, trailing the van from a greater distance than before, its headlights off.

The aquarium was a 1930s art-deco style whitewashed building nestled beside a small, two-screen cinema and a bank. Josh had been expecting something grander; a more dominating building, something that would have outclassed its counterpart in Edinburgh, but instead, he looked at the building and could only think that it was....

"A hole – a right hole. What would they bring her here for?"

"Her?" Stovey snorted. "How do you ken it's a she dalfin? No wonder you're so bothered. Are you trying to get it together?"

"Shut your stupid yap," Josh snapped. Angus intervened and held a finger to his mouth as he stared at Stovey.

"Ach, all right. I was only guising," Stovey apologised. The van came to a halt at the side of the aquarium building. Around 150 metres behind the tailing car, its lights off, pulled up softly next to the kerb and Maxine killed the engine. She and Suzy stared through the windscreen at the van ahead.

"Now what? Maxine asked, stifling a yawn.

"We wait," replied Suzy.

Gaining entry to the aquarium was easier than Josh, Stovey, and Angus had imagined. Between the old cinema and the aquarium there was a dark alley where they found an emergency fire door. Angus shoved the door open. There were no alarms, no security lights, no guards. It was almost too good to be true. Things had gone so smoothly, but Josh wasn't willing to push his luck. He insisted they retreat to the doorway of the neighbouring cinema and watch the now opened rear door and listen. Fifteen minutes elapsed before the reality seeped in and it became clear there was going to be no security response. There was no sign of any police.

"The coast's clear. They're no coming. Who would want to guard a crummy place like this anyway?" Stovey concluded. There was barely a sound in the night air. The building afforded a degree of protection from the northeasterly wind, but the chill still clawed at Josh's ears as he stepped out of the doorway shadow and onto the rough ground that led back into the dark alley and the open emergency door.

"Right, let's go. Keep a listen out for the horn."

Josh had instructed Peter to stay in the van. With the driver's window partially open he was to listen out for the arrival of any vehicles, ready to give a warning blast on the horn.

Stovey had his doubts. "How the hell's he gonna know if there's any cops turning up. He cannae see."

"He's got better hearing than any of us, he'll ken," Josh replied. The battery in his torch was growing weak, the circle of light it illuminated was growing smaller by the minute and almost disappeared by the time they were through the open door. Inside, Josh searched for a light switch, running the palm of his hand around the wall. Angus did the same on the opposite side. Of course it had to be Stovey who found the light switch first, clicking it on, smirking and rubbing his cheek all at the same time. Josh felt a slap was called for, but the back of his hand and Stovey's face were too far apart.

The layout of the interior was messy and shoddy. Any illusion that the facility was a match for Edinburgh has been shattered, and yet it was still the place that 'they' have decided to send Dolly. The aquarium boasted a large tank, practically an indoor swimming pool, which was more than adequate to hold dolphins.

It was in the fourth room they searched that they found the pool, dimly lit by green emergency lighting. In the dark depths of the water there was movement. The ripples on the surface were miniscule but they betrayed the creature beneath.

"It's her. It has to be her. Find the light," Josh was standing on some steps at the side of the circular tank, which almost totally filled the room. It was the size of a tennis court and a single row of bench seating was fixed around its circular wall. Angus stood on the seating and peered into the pool as Stovey punched the light switch on the wall with the side of his fist.

"There! Do you see her?" Josh could not contain his excitement as he pointed at the dark shadow slowly circling at the bottom of the pool. It was as though just seeing Dolly again was the fulfillment of the mission. Dolly rose through the water, breaking the smooth surface with her beak and letting out a double click before submerging again.

"It's big. Are you sure we're gonna be able to carry it oot of here?" Angus asked.

"With you helping, aye."

"How are we gonna catch it? Got any bait?" Stovey stood at the foot of the tank steps looking up at Josh.

"Leave that to me," Josh answered.

"Sure, you're the boss here. It's just like, how are we gonna carry it. Fish are pretty slick, especially when they're as heavy as...."

"We'll use that stretcher," Josh interrupted as he caught sight of a rolled up stretcher against the far wall. He guessed it had been used to carry Dolly into the tank. With Angus on one end and himself and Stovey on the other they should be able to transfer Dolly from the tank to the back of the van in a matter of minutes. No sweat, well not much.

"We've still got to catch the thing. Let's get a fish from one of the other tanks to bait it," Stovey suggested enthusiastically, already walking away in search of a likely candidate.

"No," Josh shouted, a little louder than he had intended. "I'll get the dolphin onto the stretcher. First of all we need to fill the tank in the back of the van with water out of this pool. Here, grab some of the buckets over there."

They each filled two buckets apiece and carried them to the front of the aquarium, splashing drops of water along the polished floor as they went. The main door was still locked. Stovey put down his buckets, and with a flex of wire and a wide grin he opened the door. Then the hard work began – a seemingly never-ending stream of journeys back and forth from the pool to the van with buckets of water for the dolphin tank. Josh felt as though his arms were going to drop off. It took almost an hour to fill the transportation tank.

"Right, that'll do it," Josh announced as Angus tipped in the final bucket.

Peter was standing on the pavement at the rear of the van smoking a cigarette. "You'll be needing me to help with the dolphin?"

"No. You stay here and look after the van and let us ken if anyone turns up nosing aboot. Angus and Stovey, you hang on here while I sort out the dolphin and the stretcher," ordered Josh.

"What, on your own?" Stovey was incredulous.

"Aye, I need to be alone. Dinnae come back until I tell you. I don't want you scaring her when I'm trying to coax her."

Stovey and Angus exchanged a glance. Stovey raised his eyebrows high.

"Now, remember. Stay oot until I call youse," Josh repeated and then disappeared back into the darkened building. In the big room he closed the door behind him and waited a moment, allowing the silence to wash over him. The only sound was the low hum of a heating element above the massive tank and a water filter bubbling softly at the far edge. He climbed the steps to the top of the pool and dipped his fingertips into the water, agitating them back and forth to attract Dolly's attention. She swam past, a few inches from him, and then circled to the far side of the pool.

"Dolly, it's me. I've come to rescue you. Can you understand?"

Dolly circled again, her dorsal fin breaking the surface as she approached Josh's hand, touching it with the tip of her beak before vanishing completely beneath the water and going further down until she was just a dark shape near the bottom of the 15-foot deep tank.

"Come on, Dolly. We've no much time. Dae yi want to get back with the others or no?"

There was a sudden splash as something broke through the surface at the far side. But it is not a dolphin that stared at Josh – it was Dolly. Her long blond hair was wet and straggly against her skin. She looked up from the edge of the pool.

"Why did you let them take me away?" she asked.

"Dolly, I couldnae stop them. They tricked me. They took you when I was away. I was let down by someone I thought I could trust."

Dolly contemplated her surroundings. "And now. Now what is to become of me in this prison?"

Josh sensed her unease. "You're better. They've given you some medicine. They've cured whatever it was that was harming you, whatever the virus was."

Dolly was silent. The ripples on the surface of the tank had all but vanished and it was as still as an undisturbed, underwater cave.

"But at what cost. What good is my health if I'm lost and trapped in captivity?"

"Aye, but you're no lost. That's why I'm here. I've got friends to help me. We can take you back tonight – in a tank of waater – and set you free into the sea in the morning."

Dolly looked straight him. "The others will have gone…"

"No they havnae. It's today. You told me they wouldn't go until this day. All we've got to do is get you back up to Edinburgh before the end of the day and back into the waater."

Dolly's eyes began to sparkle, reflecting back the lights on the ceiling, which had faded her blue pupils to the colour of a distant horizon on a cloudless summer's day. "By today? This is the last day. If I'm not back in the sea I will be lost to the others. I won't be able to find my way back without them."

"You have to trust me Dolly. I'll get you back in time. You have to get onto this stretcher here so that we can carry you out of here." Josh stepped down from the side of the tank and retrieved the stretcher from where it was propped against the wall. He placed it beside the door. There was a cascade of water as Dolly climbed from the tank and slowly descended the metal access steps. Her wet hair stuck to her naked body. Josh was mesmorised by her beauty. Her long, slender legs were carefully placed with each step in the elegant manner of a catwalk model. Dolly's eyes focued on the yellow plastic of the stretcher and its two carrying poles on either side. She flicked her eyes at Josh.

"And you can get me there before dawn?"

Josh nodded.

"Your friends, do they know about me?"

"In the name of....." Suzy's banshee cry echoed through the room as she lunged forward, pulling at Dolly's long hair, yanking her to the floor screaming in pain. "Yi slut, I've got you now," she pulled Dolly back onto her knees and started to drag her backwards. Dolly struggled, trying to free herself, but it was to no avail. Her assailant had a tight grip on her hair.

"Suzy, let her go." Josh jumped forward to pull the women apart. His first effort failed and he fell to the floor as Suzy's rage took over and she half swung the naked Dolly around by her hair. Josh regained his feet and advanced again, but Suzy stared him down as she tightened the pull on the incapacitated Dolly, who screamed with pain.

"Back off Josh, or I'll really hurt her," Suzy's words are cold and measured as though some automation had taken over her emotions. Josh froze midstep.

"Suzy. You don't understand."

"What don't I understand? I don't understand that you bring this slut back home with you from the pub? I don't understand that you drive half way in England to see her and I catch you naked. I don't understand? You're damn right I don't."

"I'm no naked," he corrected.

"No, but she is," Suzy yanked at Dolly's hair again, Dolly let out another painful cry. "She's helping you get that dolphin again, isn't she?"

"What?"

"I'm no daft, Josh. I've been following you all night; you, Stovey, and the others. I know they're outside waiting. You're here to get the dolphin and do...do who knows what. And this hussy's in it with you." Suzy's eyes fired with rage.

"It's no like that, Suzy listen to me," Josh pleaded.

"No, you listen to me for once."

"For once?"

"No back chat," Suzy shot back. "Your game's up. I called the animal protection just before I came in here. They know what you're up to and the polis will be here any minute. Your stupid game's over. No going to be able to act the big man any more, eh?"

Josh threw his hands against his eyes then slowly slid them apart to look at Suzy. "No... tell me you didn't. You don't know what you've done."

"I know exactly what I've done and I'm glad I came after you to see for myself what you're doing behind my back – after all these years. How long's this been going on, eh?"

But even as she spoke Suzy felt her grip on the woman's hair slipping. The hair was becoming slicker; it felt as though it was changing. In the second it took for Suzy to react and look down the woman had gone and there was a six-foot long dolphin on the floor.

"In the name of...." Suzy stepped back, unsure and looked up at Josh as though he was a witchdoctor.

"Suzy, that's what she is. She's a dolphin, no a woman."

"This shit's no real. I didn't just see that. Tell me I didn't just see that," said Suzy as she tried to catch her breath. Her heart was racing.

"It's real, trust me."

Suzy stared into Josh's eyes. "Josh, you're mental."

"Look, none of the others ken. They just think it's a dolphin. We've got to get her back to the Forth."

"Josh, what's going on?" Suzy's voice quivered with fear.

"She's a dolphin. What you just saw is what I saw. She's a dolphin. She came to me at Cramond and asked for help. That's what I've been doing," Josh replied. "I once saved her and she needs my help again. Don't ask me how this happens, because I don't know."

Suzy shook her head in disbelief and ran a hand through her hair. "This is too weird. You cannae keep this a secret. They'll want to find out about this and do experiments and stuff."

"That's why I'm no telling anyone. She's going back into the water and no-one is going to know." Josh's face was pleading. "Suzy, now that you know, you've got to be on my side or this is all for nothing."

The sound of running footsteps echoed through the room. Angus and Stovey appeared at the door.

"What's all the noise?" Angus asked in a loud whisper before he and Stovey halted in their tracks at the sight before them.

"What the…Suzy?" Stovey blurted

"Join the party boys. It's just getting interesting," Suzy had regained her composure.

"Suzy's here," Josh stated the obvious. "Look, there's no time to explain. We've got to get this dolphin back into the water fast or she'll die. You two give me a hand to roll her onto the stretcher and get her to the van." He turned to Suzy. "You can help if you want. It's up to you what you do now."

Suzy remained frozen, watching as the other three moved the stretcher to the floor beside the dolphin and rolled the creature onto it. Angus took up the two carrier poles at one end, while Josh and Stovey took one apiece at the other. They begin to walk, almost in step, out of the room and towards the front of the building.

Suzy stood alone and unsure. She thought about Maxine, half asleep in the car further along the street keeping watch. She thought about the voice message she had left on the SSPCA women's phone before following Josh and the others into the aquarium. Then, with hesitant steps, she followed the others.

Lifting and carrying the dolphin proved more of a struggle and hardship than Josh had anticipated. Angus, bringing up the rear, was the only one who seemed at ease with the task. Josh could feel his knees buckling and saw the strain on Stovey's face as they exited the aquarium and reached the van, hoisting the dolphin upwards and into the back of the van. With one final burst of energy they lifted the stretcher high enough to roll the dolphin into the tank of water secured inside. They watched as it splashed and came to animated life in the tight confines of its new temporary home. Angus and Stovey were unable to take their eyes off the creature, staring intently at the eye on its left side that looked back at them.

Suzy had slipped away unseen, jogging up the road to Maxine's car, but she had not disturbed her sleeping friend. Instead, she returned to stand a few feet from the back of the van outside the aquarium.

"Right, let's get going. We've wasted too much time already," Angus said as he and Stovey backed off and jumped down from the van. Josh followed them down to where they stood next to Suzy.

"No we're no," Josh corrected Angus.

Stovey's eyes narrowed. "What dae yi mean, no? There's still a couple of hours of darkness, we can be well up the road before a soul kens we've been."

"They already know what we're up to, and they probably know we've got this van too," Josh explained, turning to Suzy. "That's right, eh?"

Suzy bowed her head. "Aye. I called the polis before I followed you into the building."

"Shit!" said Stovey. "So what are we doing having a mothers' union meeting oot here. Let's get the fuck oot."

"Hang on. They'll know this is the van they're looking for; it'll no take a Sherlock Holmes to deduce that. So the road back is going to be full of fuzz searching for us," said Josh.

They hadn't noticed Blind Peter climb out of the van cab, but he now made his presence known. "That's true, especially a van like this. Did you say it had a seal on the side?"

Josh had momentarily forgotten about the bold advertising décor. "Fuck. That's it. We'll never get back in this thing. Look at it," he led the others around to the side of the van and pointed up at the brightly coloured picture of Sammy the Seal advertising Edinburgh Aquarium, splashed along the side.

Angus rubbed his beard. "Aye, it's a bit of a giveaway."

CHAPTER SIXTEEN

IT'S PINK, MAN!

Katrina finished her phone conversation and pressed the disengage button on her mobile. The flat was silent, as silent as it always was at three in the morning – almost. Lisa was stirring in her bedroom and putting on her nightgown. From the living room Katrina could see a sliver of light from the partially opened door of her flatmate's room. A moment later a bleary-eyed Lisa emerged, rubbing her eyes.

"What's up?" she asked, her voice barely audible.

"Josh is trying to get the dolphin back."

"What, how?" Lisa sat down on the sofa beside the pajamas-clad Katrina.

"His ex left me a message. She's followed him down to Scarborough. They've taken a van from the aquarium."

"They?" Lisa probed.

"Some friends of his."

"How did they know where to go?"

Katrina shrugged. "Anyhow, I've called the police. Who knows what he is up to."

"And you say you know this heidcase?"

"Used to," Katrina sighed. "I used to know him. I'm not so sure now."

"So now what?" Lisa asked.

"We wait to hear if they've stopped him."

"And his ex. Is she still there?"

Katrina flicked her mobile phone back to life and scrolled down to the last received number, hitting the redial.

≈

If there hadn't been much room in the front of the van before, there was none now. Suzy sat across the laps of Stovey and Peter, Angus was hunched up in the middle crushing against Josh who barely had room to grip the steering wheel.

"One of us should have gone in the back," Stovey complained.

"We'll sort that in a minute," Josh assured, as he swung the van around a tight bend as it cruised through the empty streets of Scarborough town centre. Suzy's mobile phone buzzed to life, playing a faintly recalled chart hit song. She looked at Josh.

"Don't answer it," he said, without taking his eyes off the road. The phone played out its approximation of the cheesy song and then fell silent as the incoming call diverted to voice mail.

They had driven for three miles when they came across open countryside and Josh hauled the steering wheel to the right into a narrow dirt track. The headlights picked out a wooden fence and telegraph poles stretching into the darkness. He dropped into first gear as the van jolted up and down in the ruts and potholes along the country track.

"Is this your idea of a short cut?" Stovey piped up.

"This should do nicely," Josh eased the van into an even narrower spur track, which led to a thicket of trees and bushes. He gently applied the brakes, bringing the van to a halt and switching off the ignition. The lights went out and the darkness of night consumed everything outside the windows.

"Now what?" Stovey asked.

"We wait."

"For what? I thought you said we had to get this dalfin back pronto."

"We wait here until daybreak and then we make a few changes to disguise the van," Josh replied. "I suggest we spread out here and in the back and get some sleep. Then we'll make our next move."

After only three hours of fitful rest the five gathered at the back of the van. In the thin light of dawn, Dolly the dolphin rested near the bottom of the tank, rising once in a while to take a breath of air. But Dolly was not the centre of attention; it was Josh who was holding forth. He knew his idea was going to cause conflict between himself and Stovey, and he wasn't disappointed. The idea of walking on foot back to Scarborough, having driven a few miles out of the town boundaries, did not go down well. The suggestion of finding a scrap yard to pinch some car number plates to swap with those on the van was laughed at – but Stovey's laughter dried up when Josh gave him his own individual mission.

Three hours later Suzy watched as Josh lay on his back on the uneven wild, grassy ground and started to clumsily unbolt the number plates from the van. On the grass next to him was a set of new plates he had liberated from an old wrecked car abandoned by the side of the road. They had come across the wreck as they had walked back to town earlier that morning.

On the walk Josh had tried to explain what had happened, why he had brought the dolphin home, how it had appeared to him as a woman stranded on the beach. He'd even related back to the childhood incident on the beach with Katrina and the baby dolphin.

Suzy had taken it all in. She had asked some questions, but had stayed unusually quiet, weighing up all she was being told. During the morning her mobile phone had rung a few times. She followed the instruction not to answer it. Three of the calls had come from Katrina, asking if there was any update and where was she, where was the van, where was the dolphin? There had also been two calls from Maxine, who had awoken in her car to the sound of a police officer tapping on the window. She noticed the van had gone and so had Suzy. Police had swarmed around the front of the aquarium with flashlights blazing. Maxine had played dumb and then driven off, searching for any sign of the van on the road as she headed back to Scotland.

Suzy had not responded to any of the messages. She watched Josh working on the number plates. Angus and Stovey had been sent on their own mission to find paint, but had not returned. Blind Peter had been assigned the task of looking after the van while everyone else was gone. He was sitting on a rock near the front of the van, feeling the warmth of the late morning sunshine filtering through the branches of the trees.

Josh got to his feet, brushing grit and dirt from his shirt. He was aware once more of the sound of traffic on the nearby main road, although the trees that obscured the van from view acted as a partial sound buffer.

It was eleven in the morning by the time Stovey and Angus returned from their errand. Josh watched them approach. They had traipsed all the way back to the town and waited until a large hardware store opened up for the day. Beads of sweat glistened on their foreheads as they dropped eight cans of five litres of paint on the ground. Angus placed four broom handles and roller brushes on the ground beside the tins of paint. "I'm knackered," he announced, straightening his back.

"Aye, you and me both," Stovey chipped in. "Dae yi ken how far that bloody place is? Five miles – five bleeding miles, that's ten there and back." Josh ignored the exaggeration and crouched beside the paint, pulling out a penknife to prise open one of the lids.

"What fucking colour's this?" His jaw dropped.

"Don't knock it. It was cheap. Have you any idea how much this stuff costs normally," Stovey replied.

"It's bloody pink, man!" Josh couldn't believe his eyes.

"It's rose," Stovey corrected, rubbing his bare forearms across his sweating brow.

"My arse, it's pink, man! Can you no see that?"

"Whit does it matter as long as it covers up Sammy the fucking seal."

"Stovey, the hail idea was that we made the van less conspicuous, no a bleedin' freak mobile."

Suzy giggled and turned away. Blind Peter had left his rock and now stood hitching his underpants, as he did so he breathed in deeply, his string vest-shrouded chest expanding. "We've no time to argue. It feels like it's getting near tay noon and we've got to get the dolphin back to the sea before this evening, is that no right?" he said.

"Aye it is, Peter," Josh reluctantly agreed and grabbed a roller brush to fix onto the edge of one of the broom handles.

Angus tipped the open can of paint into one of the three plastic trays that Stovey had bitched about carrying for the past hour and a half. "Doesn't look too bad when it's spread a bit," he said hopefully.

If Stovey had bitched about having to carry the paint and trays on the walk back from town, it was nothing to the way he bitched as he slapped the paint onto the side of the van. With four of them working, and Peter whistling to himself as he caught a tan from the midday sun, the paint job did not take long. Sammy the Seal and all mention of the Edinburgh Aquarium were soon obliterated by pink paint. It was hardly a neat job, but Angus repeatedly assured that the paint would settle into a nice coat once fully dry. There was barely a drop of paint to spare. Stovey was delighted. "Job done, let's hop it," he slapped his palms together.

Josh was just as eager to get moving. It was past one in the afternoon and time was running away from them. Getting back to the Forth before night was going to take a non-stop effort, and it was with such pressing thoughts whirling around his head that he crunched the gears as he searched for reverse and moved the van out of its hiding place amongst the trees and back along the country track to the main road. There was more room in the front cab of the van; Suzy and Peter had volunteered to sit in the back with the dolphin tank.

"No a bad effort, even if I do say so myself," Stovey congratulated, winding down the passenger window to gain some fresh air. He let one of his fingers run along the fresh paintwork on the side of the door as the countryside whizzed past at a steady 52 miles per hour. "Still tacky," he announced, inspecting his finger, which was now daubed a tasteless shade of pink.

"It'll be dry soon enough if we keep this pace up," Josh predicted, his foot pressing the accelerator pedal hard.

"Yi ken, sometimes I amaze even myself by how ingenious I can be," Stovey plucked up.

"Hey, dinnae bust your arm patting yourself on the back. Let's remember whose idea it wis," said Josh.

"Am no saying it wis just me. We all played a part. Teamwork," Stovey finished off.

"So, are we going to make it back in time?" asked Angus, sitting between them.

"I think we'll just do it, if there are no hold ups." Josh could sense the mid-afternoon sky was darkening by the minute as they headed north. The bright sunshine of Scarborough had dissipated with the miles, and two hours into the journey the sky had turned to a dull grey. Spots of rain begin to hit the windscreen, tiny droplets too small and infrequent to justify using windscreen wipers, but annoying all the same. If the rain started now Josh would be forced to slow down and that could tip the delicate balance over whether they would make it back to Edinburgh during daylight and in time for Dolly to be reunited with her pod. If that was not a worrying enough concern, a figure dressed in black and fluorescent green on the road ahead was the last thing that he, Stovey and Angus wanted to see.

"The fuzz, that's all we need. How do they ken it's us? We've changed the number plates, painted the...." Stovey began, but was cut off by Angus' deep voice.

"They don't know, they cannae. It must just be a routine check."

Angus was right, Josh told himself as he crunched back down the gears and brought the van to a halt in a lay-by next to the policeman who was standing a few feet out in the carriageway of the road with his arm raised and outstretched.

"Can I help, officer?" Josh said as he lowered the window. He could see the parked police car further along in the lay-by, and another patrol officer standing at the far side of it putting on a bright, luminous waterproof jacket.

"Would you mind switching off the engine and stepping out of the vehicle, sir," requested the first officer. The rain was falling harder. Had he still been driving Josh would have now needed the windscreen wipers. As soon as he jumped down from the van he felt the cold water beating against his head and face. He followed the policeman to the back of the van. The officer was young, maybe early 20s, and he held a small notebook into which he was writing details as he checked the van. Was he writing down the number plates? Would he compare them to the vehicle licensing authority records and discover they belonged to a Ford Fiesta car? Josh felt a trickle of uncomfortable sweat running down the nape of his neck.

"Your vehicle, sir?" the officer half-stated as he looked up from his notepad. His colleague had walked around to the side of the van and was watching from a few feet away.

"Aye," Josh replied.

"And where are you heading?"

"Glasgow."

"Live there do you?"

"Aye."

"And where have you been?"

"Leeds, helping a pal moving his furniture. We're just on our way back hame." The rain was beating harder, as though God had turned a knob from three to eight in one swift movement. Josh let his eyes fall to the ground as he prayed that he won't be asked to open up the back of the van. As he examined his all too familiar scuffed and worn shoes he saw a puddle of water forming where the rain was running off a corner of the van. The water was a shade of oily pink. In terror, he shifted his gaze upwards and saw the paint along the side of the van beginning to run. It was thinning out. The red ball and the snout of Sammy the Seal were barely covered and with each passing second the battering rain washed away more of the paint.

A sheet of rain smacked into the side of the van and the police officer with the notebook shut it tight and hurriedly crammed it into his jacket pocket, then he looked at Josh. "The reason I've stopped you is that we're looking for a box van that was stolen from Edinburgh yesterday and might be used to steal….a dolphin," he said, lowering his voice at the end.

On cue Josh dropped his jaw and mimicked an incredulous laugh. "A dolphin?" He was acutely aware of where he was focusing his eyes and forced them away from the rapidly vanishing paint job on the side of the van. "That's pretty mental. What would anyone want with a dolphin?"

"No idea," the officer pulled the front of his cap lower so that it almost covered his eyes. "But they're not very bright. They stole a van from another aquarium with its name all over it."

Josh tried his hardest to laugh naturally, but was deeply self-conscious that he might sound phony. "What a bunch of planks. Well, I'll keep my eyes oot for them," he smiled.

"Much appreciated," said the officer.

With measured steps Josh turned and walked back to the front of the van. His eyes flicked upwards to the side of the van as he passed. Sammy the Seal was now clearly visible beneath the thinnest covering of paint as the bucketing rain pummeled the side panels. He took two more steps, hopped into the cab and shut the door. Rain rattled against the windows as he started the ignition and glanced in the side mirror. The two police officers were still standing at the back of the van in the downpour.

"Where did you get that paint?" Josh asked without taking his eyes from the road as the van pulled away.

"What's up?" Stovey replied.

"You didnae get it in a shop, did yi."

"It did the job, so is doesn't matter where it came fae."

"That's the point, it bloody well does," Josh diverted his eyes from the road and looked across at Stovey and Angus. "The rain washed it straight off."

Stovey sighed. "It was a knockdown price. The fella gave us a bargain. If the rain is washing it off that's because we didn't gie it enough time to dry. There's nowt wrong with the paint."

It was raining harder now, pelting straight against the windscreen so strongly that the wipers could no longer keep pace. Josh grunted and ordered the others to look for a turning where they could get off the road and park out of sight until the rain slowed.

Angus noticed another farm track and Josh swung the van sharply down the muddy track until they had gone 100 metres, then he pulled up and switched off the engine. The battering of the rain against the windows and the aluminium roof was deafening.

"Don't look at me like that," Stovey complained from the far side of the cabin, his back pressed against the passenger door as he stared back at Josh.

"You were responsible for the paint," Josh chided.

"The paint was fine. It looked fine. It didn't dry enough."

"It was indoor paint. No wonder the rain washed it off," Josh was doing a bad job at controlling his rising temper.

"That's no what it said on the tins. The guy who sold it…."

Josh jumped in again. "What! So you didn't even buy it in a shop?"

Stovey swallowed. "No. There was…"

"There was this guy doing a building job at a house and Stovey cut a deal," Angus explained.

Josh let the facts sink in. "Cut a deal. Great. You cut another dodgy deal and we're in this mess." He looked out through the windscreen where the rain was pumping harder and the glass was steaming up, obscuring the outside world.

"How was I to ken?" Stovey protested.

"S'right Josh. The paint was in the wrong cans. We were done," Angus offered.

Josh slapped his hands on the steering wheel and gave out an exasperated sigh, "Look's like we're buggered then." He opened the door and jumped down into the rain, his worn shoes sinking into a muddy puddle. "Stay here 'till I come back." He slammed the door and walked to the back of the van, stopping halfway to look up at the side where the pink paint had been washed away. Sammy the Seal was playing with his ball and Edinburgh Aquarium was inviting all to come along.

The lane they had driven onto petered out into an overgrown track of brambles. At least the van was not blocking a farm drive after all. It was a crumb of consolation for Josh. He lifted the shuttered back door of the box van. Blind Peter was sitting next to the tank, a puddle of water at his feet from where the tank water had splashed over the rim during the journey. Suzy was sitting in the corner, her back wedged against the tank and the side of the van. Dolly the dolphin was hovering at mid-depth.

"We there already?" Peter asked.

"No," Josh replied as he hopped up. Suzy watched him silently and intensely. "We're no even back in Scotland yet. Got a problem with the paint job – it's all washed away." Josh walked towards the tank. "I'm going to need a few minutes here Peter. Can you go up front?"

Peter got to his feet and made his way to the back of the van, climbing down in the rain and disappearing around the side. Josh listened as the cab door opened and closed, then he pulled down the shuttered back door of the van. Suzy was still in the corner, but now she was standing. She said nothing and watched Josh, a swirl of intensity, return to the water tank. The dolphin was tightly confined; there was not enough room for her to turn around. Josh pitied her and lifted the flimsy plastic lid to peer into the water, touching its surface to create gentle ripples. The change occurred almost instantly and Dolly's wet blonde hair dangled across her eyes as she stood in the tank looking at him, then she glimpsed Suzy. Her eyes widened in fear.

"It's okay," Josh reassured.

Dolly looked back at him, sensing his sadness.

"It's no going to work," he said. "We've tried our best. But there's no way we can get you back up in time, not before tonight."

"What's happened?" Dolly asked in a whisper.

"We needed to disguise the van, paint it another colour so that it wouldn't be recognised," Josh lifted his eyes towards the grey light filtering through the Perspex ceiling as rain pounded above. "Then the rain washed it all off. If we try and drive the rest of the way we'll be stopped by the first police car that clocks us."

"Can't you paint it again?"

"Aye, but not now. Not while it's raining. We'd have to wait for it to dry off and then go and fetch paint from who knows where. We're in the middle of nowhere and it'll be dark in about four hours."

"We won't be there until night?"

"Not until sometime tomorrow – probably morning at the earliest even if we manage to paint the van."

With the gentlest of movements, hardly disturbing the water she was standing in, Dolly lifted a hand and brushed some stray strands of hair away from her eyes. "Then the others will be gone."

"Are you sure they'll no wait?"

Dolly shook her head. "If they wait until last light this evening they might stay the night. It is difficult to travel by night, but….if they do, then they will leave as soon as day breaks. They will not stay any longer, it would be too much of a risk."

Josh turned and walked the three steps to the back of the van as Dolly and Suzy watched. For a moment he stared into the dirt encrusted slats of the shuttered door. His mind was hundreds of miles away, already it had reached the beach at Cramond. He could taste the salt spray against his lips, whipped from the uneven surface of the Firth of Forth. It was only a few hundred miles away, a couple of hours at the most. Yet it might as well be on the other side of the world. He put his hands on his hips and turned.

Dolly stood still in the tank, her hair cascading over her shoulders and reaching halfway down her body. Her golden locks shrouded her eyes, which intently watched Josh. Her lips were slightly open as though she was about to speak.

"I'm sorry," Josh filled the moment, although his words were almost drowned out by the thumping rain against the roof. "I've failed you this time. I shouldn't have been so dumb. This was never going to happen. If I hadn't trusted her." An image of Katrina flashed across his mind.

"You've done more than I expected and I thank you for that," Dolly said. Josh felt compelled to walk towards her as though summoned. He stopped when his shoe touched the edge of the tank. His face was only a few inches from hers. Now he was close enough to see her blue eyes beyond the unruly fringe, and they sparkled in the semi-light. She lifted her right arm. Josh felt the soft touch of her hand against his shoulder, as light as a butterfly alighting. Their eyes locked, and then Josh slowly pulled away and walked to the back of the van again and slid the roller door up, jumping down into the rain and closing the door behind him.

Dolly and Suzy were alone. The only sound was the pummeling rain against the roof. Dolly's eyes were fixed on the back door of the van, as though she expected Josh to return at any moment. Suzy shuffled forward.

"I'm sorry for the way I acted earlier," she said.

The words jolted Dolly from her trance-like state. She looked at Suzy. "You weren't to know what was going on. It was a natural reaction."

"No, it was a dumb reaction," Suzy said. "I hurt you."

"I've had worse," Dolly smiled.

"I know. Josh told me the story earlier today," Suzy continued. "I wish he'd told me it a long time ago, instead of keeping it hidden away. I wished he'd shown me this other side."

Dolly again pushed some strands of hair away from her eyes. "He feels he's failed you, and himself." She looked away. "And now me."

"How do you mean?"

Dolly locked her eyes back on Suzy's. "The way he drinks, the way he's lost faith in himself and become a burden."

"He's told you that?"

"Some of it; the bits he's prepared to put into words. The other things are unspoken, repressed." Dolly paused, a small smile appeared. "But not very well."

Suzy looked away, allowing the words to sink in. Dolly continued, "He's broken and he's trying to fix himself. All this has put him back in touch with who he once was. It has given him a purpose, a chance to do something good. To prove himself."

"To me?" Suzy turned to face Dolly.

"To himself first, and then to you, and the world. When he's found reason again to love and respect himself, only then will he feel worthy of giving and receiving love."

"You think?" Suzy said.

"I know," Dolly answered, as she began to lower her head and shoulders into the water as though sensing something. "Right now he feels everything is slipping away from him."

The sound of the rain against the roof of the van had diminished to a tiny pitter-patter. There was a heavy rap against the shuttered back door. Suzy jumped and looked at the door and then back at the tank. Dolly had submerged and was once more a dolphin, floating mid-depth in the water. Suzy lifted the shutter door. Angus and Stovey were standing outside in the gossamer drizzle that had replaced the cloudburst.

"Is Josh there?" Angus asked.

Suzy shook her head, then noticed Josh further along the muddy track walking back towards the van. "There he is," she pointed.

The promise of sunshine was emerging from the clouds. "What's up?" Josh asked as he approached the van.

"We can go and get some more paint," Stovey suggested.

"What time is it?" said Josh.

"Half-four," Angus' deep voice rumbled.

"We'd be lucky to find some place open. We must be miles from the nearest town," Josh said. Suzy jumped down, her eyes intently watching Josh.

"There looks to be a housing estate over there," Angus pointed towards some wet rooftops that sparkled in the weak rays of the breaking sun. "Probably only a mile and a half."

"Still too far," said Josh, pulling the shutter door of the van shut.

"So that's it then. We're no going to try anymore?" Stovey kicked a stone despondently.

"We'll wait until dark and then drive through the night. There's less chance we'll be spotted," Josh said.

"Will that no be too late?" Angus grunted, pulling at his beard.

"As long as we make it by dawn there's still a chance," Josh was as surprised by his optimism as anyone.

For the remainder of the evening he felt light-headed, a sensation that was heightened further by the dream-like quality of the crimson sunset on the rolling green hills to the west. Together with Angus, Stovey, Peter and Suzy he sat on the grass at the side of the van until the red sky deepened into purple. He wondered what Peter was getting out of it, unable as he was to see the heavenly colours. What was he feeling?

Without warning Peter turned his head and said, "It's a big risk to take – even in the dark. They'll be oot there looking for us. That lassie from the SSPCA you telt us aboot, she kens what you're doing."

It was a nagging doubt that Josh had tried to ignore, something he had tried to shut away, but it was true. Suzy stood up and gestured for him to follow her. They walked from the grass verge beside the van and down along the darkening track. Soon they were out of hearing range of the others.

Josh's mind was still churning. "The polis ken exactly what's going on. Peter's right, Katrina has told them."

"Were you expecting anything different?" Suzy asked. "She told me you were pals at school. But that was a long time ago, Josh. Her job is to look after the welfare of animals. It isnae to cover your arse."

Josh sighed. "She'll ken exactly where we'll be heading. She knows the beach. We're stuffed."

"And they'll be looking for the van through the night," Suzy added to the lengthening list of woe.

Josh contemplated it all for a moment. "I've still got to try. That's all I've left to do."

He walked on, not noticing that Suzy has stopped. She watched as he meandered through the thin mud of the track, head bowed in thought. All her anger and distain for his actions and his lack of actions over the years, melted away. He now had the appearance of a lost boy in the wilderness, trying to do something right but finding at ever turn he was going to be beaten for doing wrong. She saw the man she fell in love with so many years before, but older, wearier and crest-fallen, yet clinging to the last vestiges of defiance. She called to him. He had almost walked out of hearing range, almost. He turned and watched as she trotted towards him, the light of the low sun catching in her short, dyed-blonde hair.

"I'll phone her," Suzy said, as she got closer.

"Who?"

"The SSPCA woman - Katrina. I'll call her and tell her where you're heading."

"What?"

"Which beach are you going to?"

"Cramond," Josh answered, confused.

"I'll tell her it's Leith. They'll go there and wait for you."

"How are you going to convince her you know all this? She'll no believe you," Josh doubted.

"I'll tell her I'm in the van and I've heard your plan."

"And how are you in the van?"

"I'll say you've kidnapped me. Maxine's probably told the police that already, she doesn't know why I disappeared in Scarborough while she was sleeping in the car."

Josh shook his head in disbelief. "Great, now I'll get done for kidnap as well."

Suzy was already switching on her mobile phone. "Eight missed calls," she announced. "Four from Max...four from your friend." She hit the reply button.

CHAPTER SEVENTEEN

SECOND GUESSING

Another gust of wind whistled across the sandy expanse of Cramond beach as Katrina snapped her mobile phone closed. She was not alone. Around a dozen police officers were milling around, together with an assortment of SSPCA colleagues, veterinarians and a group from the British Divers Marine Life Rescue. Out in the Firth of Forth, a few hundred metres from the shore were two boats. One was a lifeguard patrol boat, the other a dive boat owned by the marine life rescuers. Two police Land Rovers were parked close to the slipway entrance to the beach.

"That was her," Katrina informed Bruce MacLeod, the SSPCA regional director. He was standing next to a police superintendent.

"Where is she?" MacLeod asked, adjusting his cap against the wind. He was in his late 50s. His bushy eyebrows had started to turn grey in sympathy with his receding hair. He had served with the animal protection organisation for more than 25 years. His blue eyes peered through small-rimmed glasses at Katrina.

"They bundled her into the van when they took the dolphin."

"They did what?" interjected the towering and slightly overweight police superintendent standing next to MacLeod.

"She's all right. They've locked her in the back of the van with the dolphin. They're keeping it in a holding tank. She said they went the wrong way, drove south and then realised their mistake and are heading north again. She heard them say they would be coming in to Edinburgh tomorrow morning, from the Portobello direction, and were intending to release the dolphin at Leith first thing."

"Leith?" MacLeod and the superintendent chimed in unison.

Katrina shrugged. "I don't get it. But she's adamant. They had her under watch until now so she couldn't call. They've left her alone in the back of the van with the dolphin."

"But why Leith? You said yourself this had to be the place," said MacLeod.

"I did, and I still believe that. But…she's been right about the other stuff, about the dolphin in the bath and about them going to Scarborough. If they think we're going to be here waiting at Cramond then maybe that's why they're going to go to Leith instead." A cold wind whipped up along the estuary and brushed the wide beach as if to warn that nightfall was on the way. Katrina shivered.

"Trying to second guess us," the police superintendent rubbed his double chin and looked at MacLeod. "What do you think?"

"It's getting late in the day if they were to attempt anything. Tomorrow morning seems more likely, and it would be a smart wee trick to go to Leith."

The superintendent nodded. "We'll station a watch overnight and redeploy. Now that we know the direction they're taking to reach the city we can set up patrols. We'll probably have them before they get anywhere near Leith," he said with confidence.

≈

One hundred and forty-seven miles away Josh and Suzy rejoined Angus, Stovey and Peter who were sitting on the grass verge beside the van.

"We'll have to make a detour, stick to the back roads," Josh announced. A strand of purple twilight streaked the western horizon and stars were beginning to appear one by one in the clearing sky. A chill cloak of air was descending, and in the vale between the houses a fine white mist rose like a ghost to swallow the hedgerows.

"Detour! What kind of detour?" Stovey asked with alarm. He stopped throwing stones at the wooden post five feet ahead of where he was sitting and turned to Josh and Suzy.

"We cannae go back up the same road. They'll be expecting us to take the direct route. We need to find a different way in, something that'll take us into Edinburgh from a totally different direction, and we cannae use the main roads either," Josh explained.

Angus was on his feet, stretching his back with his arms reaching upwards as though he were a giant bear awakening from hibernation.

"What are you proposing?" he asked.

Josh had barely considered his plan, but he answered swiftly to convey a sense of control and planning and lull the others into thinking he had it all worked out. "Glasgow. We'll heed for Glasgow and then turn in to Edinburgh from the west."

"Glasgay! Are you aff your heid? That'll take us all fucking night," Stovey chucked the remainder of his stones in one mass flurry at the wooden post, scoring one clunking strike to double his score of the past half hour. He was on his feet and squared up to Josh. "Does it no occur to you that some of us need to get to oor beds. We've already been one night without sleep and noo you want to drive all night to get to Glasgay on the way to Edinburgh," Stovey gave the side of his own head an exaggerated punch.

"The alternative is to go back the way we came and end up being banged up by the polis, because they know what way we're likely to be coming from. Is that whit you want?" Josh shot back.

Stovey shook his head but said nothing. Peter was the last of the trio to stand. He hitched his underpants. "It's a good idea, Josh. But it will take an awful lang time to get hame, so the sooner we set off the better."

Josh strode to the front of the van. He was expecting more fireworks from Stovey, but they didn't come. Angus was in step behind him and put his arm out across Josh's chest before he could climb into the driver's seat.

"Do you no want someone else to have a go at the driving? You've done plenty all ready," Angus said.

"I'm fine. I ken the way where we're going," Josh replied.

Suzy got into the back of the van to sleep.

They were back on the road. At the next junction Josh turned left and headed onto a minor road and through a string of dark, one-pub villages. Stovey had found a map book in the glove compartment and spread it out across his lap, reading off the names of the otherwise anonymous villages as they passed through them. And so it continued for a number of hours, until...

"Fuck!" The pages of the map book were furtively rifled through. Stovey repeated his exclamation. "Pages are missing!"

"What?" Josh took his eyes off the narrow country road.

"We've no fallen off the map?" Angus asked. His hand reached out to touch the map book as if doing so might help find the missing pages.

"There's a whole stack of pages missing fae the centre," said Stovey. Josh applied the brakes and brought the van to a halt in the middle of the road. The pitch black of night had swallowed the world outside, while the illuminated clock on the dashboard informed him it was four minutes past midnight. He reached across for the map book, which Stovey handed over without argument. It only took a second to see that a number of pages have been ripped out.

"Now what do we do? We're going to have to start following the signposts back to Edinburgh," Stovey concluded.

"Ahem," Peter cleared his throat. He has been asleep for the past few hours, his quiet but audible snoring like a metronome as the hours had ticked by. "Where did we last pass through?"

Stovey scratched his head. "Ripleston," he answered

"Right. Then we carry on straight."

"Peter, what are you saying? Do you know this area?" It seemed a ridiculous question to ask a blind man, but Josh asked all the same.

"I'll find the way."

"Peter, we don't have the time to end up getting anymore lost than we already are. We need to get there..." Josh began.

"By first light. And we will. Straight on. I'll tell yi when to turn." When Peter spoke everyone listened, that had always been the way for as long as any of the other three could remember. However, Josh now wanted to question his judgment, but with no past reference of a bad decision to compare to he was lost. The night beckoned, blind faith led the way.

As the miles went by they visited more than a dozen sleeping villages and towns. At each junction Josh asked which way and Peter responded with a left here a right here, although mostly it was an instruction to carry on straight ahead. Josh's feeling of unease increased the further they went. The dashboard clock seemed to have sped up. It was approaching three in the morning. There would be no chance of making it to Edinburgh in time for the first light if they had made a mistake on the road. They did not have the luxury of any spare time.

Then one of the wheels fell off the wagon.

Josh had not noticed his eyelids becoming heavier, or the increasing time they took to open and close each time he blinked. He was unaware they had blinked closed and not reopened until the van juddered and shook. Angus' huge hands reached across and grabbed the steering wheel as Josh's eyes opened in time to see an embankment loom up through the arc of the headlights. A stonewall scraped the nearside of the van. There was a crunch and squeal. The front of the van lifted into the air for a moment and then was jolted back onto the ground, skidding. Josh had his foot planted on the brake pedal, but he could see the bus stop pole ahead looming larger and larger. There was no way the van would come to a halt in time. As the green-painted pole was struck, it bent away from view like the shaft of a plant being pushed asunder. The van stopped with a mechanical moan. Josh stared at the black of night outside.

"Let's see what the damage is," Angus released his grip on the steering wheel. Stovey opened the passenger door and jumped down to inspect the front of the van. Angus followed.

"I must have fallen asleep," Josh rubbed his head as he stood in front of the headlights, which were still beaming brightly. The nearside quarter of the van has been badly dented by the impact, but the damage did not appear so severe that it would stop them continuing the journey. Josh sighed with relief.

"Nice driving; now you've got a problem," Suzy's voice broke in from behind. Josh felt tension shaking him back to reality. He took a side step to see what Suzy had spotted at the side of the van. She was pointing at the front left wheel. "Tyre's burst."

Josh wanted to sit on the ground and hold his head in his hands. There was no way they'd make it back to the Forth before dawn. Why had he taken such a crazy route back anyway? If he had only stuck to the straight route and taken his chances with the police, he thought as he stared at the tyre. It was as deflated as his spirit, and in his tired state he was unable to put two useful thoughts together.

Angus had gone. When he returned he had a wheel brace. Stovey followed close behind with the spare wheel, which had been strapped to the underside of the van.

"Well, that's half the job. All we need now is to find a way of jacking up the front so I can get the wheel aff," said Angus, letting the wheel brace drop with a clatter on the road.

"There's no jack in the back?" Josh asked. Angus shook his head. A jack – where would they find a jack to lift the van at this time of night in the middle of nowhere? Josh scanned the surroundings and saw only darkened fields and the section of country road illuminated by the headlights of the van. There was no sign of habitation anywhere.

"We'll just have to use that post you loosened up back there," Angus remained unfazed by the situation and smiled to Josh before going to retrieve the uprooted bus stop pole and carrying it back with ease. Rocks from the damaged stonewall were gathered and used as an improvised fulcrum on which to balance the pole and create a lever strong enough to lift the front left side of the van. But almost immediately the pole began to buckle under the weight and Angus stopped his first attempt having moved the van about an inch upwards. Despite the coolness of the night sweat was beading on his forehead.

"This won't hold up for very long. You'll have tae pull the tyre off real fast and shove the other one on as quick as you can," Angus instructed. Josh and Stovey each grabbed a side of the burst tyre and waited for Angus to press the lever down and free the wheel a few inches, enough for them to shuffle it loose and off the wheel hub. Suzy stood ready holding the spare wheel. Angus grunted as he took the strain, holding the corner of the van in midair against the pole.

"Hurry, this pole'll give way any minute," he warned. The ruined tyre was thrown unceremoniously into the verge and the spare grappled into place as Josh and Stovey joined Suzy. Angus let out another grunt as the pole surrendered and folded like a drinking straw.

"Made it!" the big man announced victoriously, extracting the now useless pole. Josh tightened the wheel nuts.

"We'll take turns with the driving. You cannae go on any more," Angus announced.

Josh stood up and nodded. "Okay. I'll get a few hours in the back. But wake me when we get near to Cramond." He followed Suzy to the back of the van, while Angus climbed into the driver's seat and Stovey and Peter returned to their places on the passenger bench next to him. Once the van started rolling Josh's eyes closed as he lay on the floor with the dolphin tank towards his head and Suzy lying a few feet away on the other side.

CHAPTER EIGHTEEN

TRICKED

Katrina moved around the flat as quietly as she could, aware that it was barely four-thirty in the morning and Lisa was still asleep in her room. She dressed into her uniform and grabbed a slice of toast while gulping down a cup of tea. Then she headed out of the flat, down the flight of stairs to the empty and silent street outside.

The drive to the city centre and then skirting around to the waterfront area of Leith took less time than she imagined. There was not a soul on the streets except for the odd refuse truck working an early morning street-cleaning shift. As she drove her mind was full of thoughts, mostly stretching back to childhood memories with Josh, those inseparable times when they lived for one another. A tear rolled from one eye as she pictured their adventures and thought again about the day on the beach when they had rescued the stricken dolphin from the thuggish boys. And now there was today, more than twenty years later, and another dolphin. But this time she and Josh were on different sides. What was he trying to do? Was he really so screwed up by his waster lifestyle that he would commit such a pointless, dangerous stunt? And why?

The questions collided like driverless freight trains in her head. She shook her jet-black hair to try to throw them off, but it was no good, the same thoughts and questions came buzzing back. By the time she pulled up at Leith waterfront she was more confused than when she had left the flat. It was still night. There was perhaps another hour of darkness before first light, but already the place looked busy. A few police cars were parked at random angles. There was a Royal National Lifeboat Institute boat moored up, and Katrina recognised the British Divers Marine Life Rescue boat nearby. She wondered if any of them had gone home last night to get some sleep.

The police superintendent met her.

"We've got cars along the main Portobello roads and the routes coming in from the south. There's no way he'll slip through unnoticed," he said.

Katrina politely smiled and wandered around the waterfront, observing the activity. Now and then she stopped to check her watch. She could feel her anxiety rising as it got closer to sunrise. She returned to her car and sat inside, the driver's door slightly open so that she could hear the babbling voices of the police, the divers and the lifeboat men. She overheard the police superintendent say there was no word on the van. The sky was turning from black to an inky deep blue as the sun skulked on the fringe of the horizon as though it had lost its way. Katrina focused her attention on the highest chimney pots and awaited the reflected yellow glow to strike them and confirm the new day has arrived.

The light of day came and soon it was more than the chimney pots that were basking in the sun's rays. The pre-dawn inky blue sky diluted and refreshed to navy blue and then lighter still to an ocean hue, stretching cloudless over the city. By now Katrina was out of her car and pacing along the waterfront. The sense of anticipation that had buzzed through those assembled in the area had switched to anxiety. What was happening? Why was there no word of the van and its aquatic captive?

The police superintendent and SSPCA director, MacLeod, gathered beside Katrina. "Have you been able to contact her?" the superintendent asked, eager to know if the other captive, Suzy, could inform them about the van's location.

"I've been trying all through the night. There's no answer. Maybe her battery's flat, or they confiscated her phone," Katrina replied.

"Hmmm, maybe," said the superintendent.

"You've had no sign of the van?" Katrina asked, turning to the police chief.

"None. We've got those roads covered, there's not a chance he'd get through unseen. From Portobello right through the south of the city we're covering everything."

"It's light now. You said they were going to get here by dawn," MacLeod half-asked.

"That's what she told me. They had to be here by dawn." Katrina walked away and returned to the edge of the waterfront where the lifeboat and marine rescue boat are berthed side by side.

Something was wrong.

Something twisted in her mind, something she had just heard; something the police chief had said. She started running to the marine rescue boat and shouted for them to start the engine.

The police superintendent and MacLeod rushed across as Katrina jumped into the boat, which was now a hive of activity, as was the adjacent lifeboat.

"What is it?" MacLeod shouted.

"The west. We're watching the roads from the east and the south, but he's coming from the west. That's where Cramond is. They've tricked us," Katrina yelled back as the boat pushed off from the edge of the marina. The police superintendent had already turned away and was ordering his officers to their vehicles.

≈

A few miles away Josh rolled across the floor of the van, his head crashing against the bottom of the water tank as the vehicle came to an abrupt halt. Suzy staggered to her feet, brushing down the dirt that clung to her clothes. She watched Josh rubbing his head and his eyes, getting to his feet and yanking up the roller door. Outside, the endless sands of Cramond beach spread out as far as could be seen, one half glistening with the damp fingerprints of the retreating sea. The sun, hidden somewhere behind the van, added a dazzling brightness to everything it touched.

Angus appeared from around the side. "Eight o'clock and we're here," he announced. "Are we in time?"

Josh was groggy from lack of sleep, his movements were uncoordinated as he jumped down and surveyed the scene. The beach was almost deserted, other than two dog walkers in the distance. The tide was out. "I hope so," he answered, lifting his left arm to shield his eyes from the rising sun as he strained to see any movement in the waters of the estuary.

Suzy felt she was a mess, unbeautiful and in need of a bath. Her hair pushed out at odd angles, moulded into place while she had slept fitfully on the floor. She stood inside the van at the edge of the back door. Stovey appeared. "I think we should move a bit closer to the waater so we don't have to carry the dalfin so far," he suggested, finishing with a wide yawn.

Blind Peter was the last to arrive. He looked distracted, his head cocked upwards as though he was catching a wafting scent streaming through the air. "You best hurry lads. We're no alone," he said.

"What do you mean?" Josh asked as he, Stovey and Angus looked around at the almost empty beach.

"I dinnae see anything," Angus stated.

"Fuck...polis!" Stovey was facing inland, in the direction they had driven to get onto the beach. He pointed back along the tracks the van's wheels had made in the moist sand. In the distance two police patrol cars had come into view, klaxons screaming and red and blue lights flashing.

"And another," Josh noticed a patrol car to the east, further away than the dog walkers, but approaching rapidly. "Back in the van. Let's get her into the water."

With Suzy and Angus bracing themselves in the back, and Stovey and Peter in the passenger seats, Josh revved the engine and wheel-spun the van back to life, heading towards the receding tide. From the east the single police car headed sharply to its right in a bid to block the way. Josh swerved to avoid it and double-backed on the beach only to come face-to-face with the two patrol cars approaching from the opposite direction. He turned again and headed east with all three police cars now in a line behind. The van jolted and bumped across the sand as Josh edged it closer to the water's edge.

"Och, look up – boats!" Stovey announced as he spotted the marine rescue boat and lifeboat heading towards the beach from the east. Josh swung the van back onto softer sand and completed a near full circle, losing the police pursuers for a moment. As the van came out of its sweeping turn it was facing directly towards the cold waters of the Firth of Forth.

"What now?" asked Stovey.

"We're going to drive into the water, as far as we can get and throw the dolphin out before the fuzz reach us. You ready?"

Josh didn't wait for an answer and gunned the engine, propelling the van into the estuary until it came to a halt with four feet of water lapping around its sides. Without hesitation he, Stovey and Peter jumped down from the cab into the freezing waters, which reached up to their chests. They could see the three police cars pulling up at the edge of the sand fifty metres away, not daring to follow, but the police officers jumped out and began awkwardly wading through the shallows towards them.

Time seemed to slow down for Josh. His heart was pounding as he clambered out of the water and into the back of van where Suzy and Angus offered helping hands up for Peter, Stovey and himself. Angus took the lead and moved to the side of the tank, ready to try to tip it over.

"No," said Josh. He was at the back of the van, watching as the five wading police officers closed in. "Stop those gits from getting any nearer."

"Whit aboot the dalfin? You'll no get it oot yourself," said Stovey.

"Let me worry on that, just delay that lot," Josh pointed at the police splashing through the waist-deep water. Stovey and Angus jumped back into the water.

Peter sat down on the edge at the back of the van, "I'll no let them climb aboard," he assured.

Suzy looked at Josh, but he was already focused on the tank and its occupant. He dipped two fingers into the water and vigorously wiggled them to attract Dolly's attention. Dolly rose from the water, her lank blonde-hair cascading around her shoulders.

"There's no time left. You have to jump now, into the water. The police are right outside," Josh urged.

Dolly lifted herself clear of the tank and dropped to the floor. She held Josh for a moment and delivered a soft kiss to his left cheek. Then she turned to Suzy and said, "You are so lucky." In a blurry moment she ran three steps and jumped into the air just as she reached the back of the van. For a frozen millisecond she was both a woman and a dolphin in mid-air, then there was only a dolphin.

A few metres from the van Stovey and Angus were engaged in a messy struggle as they fought the five police officers in the water. The skirmish came to a momentary halt as all seven men turned to see the dolphin emerge from the back of the van, flying through the air and diving into the water.

"How'd he dae that?" Angus blurted, only to be brought back to reality as two police officers tackled him from the other side, pushing him headfirst into the waves.

Suzy and Josh stood at the back of the van, for a moment oblivious to the approaching police officers who had overwhelmed Stovey and Angus.

"The boats!" Suzy pointed to the two boats rapidly closing in.

From her vantage point at the bow of the marine rescue boat Katrina had a clear view of the commotion on the beach, the police chase and the officers who had grappled with the men in the water. She had watched as the dolphin dived from the van. Now she turned her attention to the orange and navy lifeboat sailing parallel about one hundred metres to port. Between the two boats stretched a fine mesh net.

"Can you see it, lassie?" the captain asked as he hung out of the cabin, raising an arm to shield from the glare of the sun dancing on the water.

"Yes, it's there, straight ahead," Katrina replied.

"And do you no think it'll be all right now it's back?" the captain shot back.

"Not on its own. Not without its pod," Katrina kept her eyes on the water.

"I see it," the captain announced as Dolly's dorsal fin broke the water and vanished again. She was heading straight between the two boats and into the net. The captain raised his arm again, this time to signal to the lifeboat to cut its engine as he switched off the rescue boat's propellers. In the sudden silence the only noise was the lapping of the water against the hull of the boat and the distant muffled cries of Stovey and Angus as they were dragged from the water to the beach, where four more police cars had lined up beside the first three.

Katrina could hear something else. There was a voice calling to her. She looked up and saw Josh and Suzy at the back of the van, and a man sitting next to them wearing only a string vest and underpants. The sitting man was yanked down into the water by one of the police officers now swarming around the half-submerged vehicle. Water was lapping above the top of the wheel arches. The police officers were clambering into the back of the van, but Josh and Suzy ignored them.

"Katrina, let her go," Josh called towards the boats before a police officer wrapped his arms around him, pinning his arms to his side then pulling him back from the edge of the van. Suzy screamed.

"Suzy, don't let them stop her," Josh pleaded. Suzy nodded. As a police officer grabbed at her jacked she slipped out of it, and in one single movement turned and dived from the edge of the van, vanishing with a splash into the murky waters of the Firth of Forth.

Even fully dressed Suzy felt the cold of the estuary chill her within seconds as she pushed through the gloomy water back to the surface. Her eyes stung from the salt. She re-orientated herself and set off with a laboured front crawl towards the nearest of the two boats. Small waves flooded her view and filled her mouth, but a determination she had long thought had deserted her took over as she ploughed through the frigid water, catching glimpses of the boats, the top of the net and the dolphin's dorsal fin.

For a moment she felt disengaged from her body. She wondered why had she not seen the genuineness of Josh's actions earlier? Why had she not sensed his noble idealism, even through the lens of his drunken stupors? Like the waves that crashed over her, so did the questioning thoughts. Her sodden clothes were dragging, tugging at her like an invisible hand trying to pull her under. But the more she felt the claws of defeat reaching out, the harder she swum.

And then she was beside the nearest of the boats. It was stationary and its white hull loomed above her. Suzy spurted salty water from her mouth as she trod water and stared up, trying to catch her breath and meeting the eyes of a dozen crewmembers. She scanned the faces and recognised Katrina.

"It's the girl they kidnapped," Katrina announced to the others. "Throw her a rope." Nearby the other boat's engine burst back to life.

"They're turning the net around in a circle, we'll have it trapped," one of the crew called out. Suzy looked across at the other boat and saw it manoeuvre forward and begin to loop back to form an arc with the outstretched net before closing in to form a circle with herself and the dolphin inside. That was clearly the intention. She turned back to the marine rescue boat. Someone threw a lifebelt down to her, but she ignored it and fixed her eyes on Katrina.

"Let the dolphin go. It's okay. Let her get through," Suzy's words were interspersed with gulps of the salty water as she struggled to keep her head clear of the waves.

"What?" Katrina called back, leaning down from the edge of the boat until she was only a few feet from Suzy.

"You've got to do it now. Let her through. Josh is right," Suzy continued to splurt. "She can make it to the others."

Katrina pushed herself away from the edge and stood upright. She heard another call from the beach and could see in the distance Josh was being hauled from the water by three police officers. He was shouting something, but he was too far away for Katrina to make out his words, except for two. "Trust me."

The lifeboat was now heading back to close up the net into a complete circle. Katrina could see the dorsal fin move back and forth as the dolphin searched for a way out, then its beak broke the surface and she saw its eye looking up at her. The dolphin squeaked twice and then vanished beneath the waves.

Maybe she was remembering something that happened many years ago. Maybe it was the salty fragrance of that same estuary that prodded her memory, or the view of that same lonely stretch of sandy beach. Maybe it was the glimpsed sight of a dolphin once more in the water and looking for safety. Or maybe it was a desire to know that someone for whom she once cared for had not become the antithesis of the beautiful soul she recognised. Whichever it was, or perhaps it was all of them, she turned around and walked five steps to where the captain was crouched, guarding the edge of the net tethered to the side of the boat.

"Any minute now, keep your fingers clear of the edge, lassie," the captain warned. But his words did not register with Katrina, all she could hear reverberating in her head were voices of a far off yesterday. The captain moved over to allow her to crouch down beside him. "That's it, we're nearly done," he said, adjusting the dusty blue skipper's cap that topped the tangled mop of white hair shrouding his head.

It was an automatic reflex. Katrina pushed the captain so that he fell backwards. She pulled at the knot that tethered the net to the boat. In a second it had unravelled and slipped into the water.

"Oh heavens, what have you done!" the captain said as he picked himself up and lunged forward to catch the end of the net as it drifted away. He was too late.

Katrina stood up and moved out of the way. She could see the crew of the other boat waving and pointing. There were a few shouts, but the words failed to register in her ears. Looking across to the water between the two boats she saw a dorsal fin rising as the dolphin arched its back and vanished beneath the waves only to reappear a few moments later on the open water side of the net. It was beyond capture.

"What have you done?" the captain repeated as he pushed himself up from the side of the boat, having been unsuccessful in his attempt to retrieve the end of the net. His eyes were accusing, but Katrina's did not meet them. Instead, her gaze was fixed to a point beyond the captain's right shoulder where the rising sun blindingly reflected back off the water. Within the brightness she saw the dolphin's dorsal fin, but this time there was another alongside, and then two more and a further flip of a dolphin's tail nearby.

"It's the pod," she said softly. The captain and crew watched in silent wonder. Two of the dolphins leapt clear from the water, curling their bodies in unison before diving beneath the waves.

The crewmembers were not the only ones watching the leaping dolphins. On the beach two police officers forced Josh to sit down on the damp sand next to Stovey, Peter and Angus. They were surrounded by police and all four had their hands cuffed behind their backs.

"Hey, look there," said one of the officers, pointing at the dolphins arching through the morning air.

Stovey moaned from the sand. "Forget that. Whit aboot these 'cuffs? They're aching man. I can get you some proper ones, job lot, nice and cheap, ken."

"Shut it," said one of the officers as he poked Stovey's right leg with the tip of his boot.

Josh strained to see the departing pod of dolphins. Sea air, droplets of salt water falling from his brow and the glare of the sun on the water were enough to cause his eyes to water.

CHAPTER NINETEEN

VISITING HOUR

The sheriff sat at the far end of the courtroom lording it on a high-backed chair. Josh kept his eyes on him, but was also aware of Stovey, Angus and Blind Peter sitting behind him on a bench. They had been dealt with, and now it was his turn.

"Mr Robertson. While your actions have been explained to this court, and the ultimate outcome accepted as a positive one, the fact remains that you broke the law. Repeatedly. However, I give credit for your guilty pleas," said the sheriff as he studied the charge sheet he had been annotating.

"For the charges of breaking and entering the aquariums, unlawfully removing a captive animal and for failing to stop when ordered to do so by a police officer, I give you the same sentence as I have given to your co-defendants. That is a one-year jail term, suspended."

Josh's eyes strayed for the shortest of moments towards the public benches on the left side of the room where Suzy and Katrina sat among a few other vaguely familiar faces. In a separate section, closer to the dock, a man and a woman were feverously scribbling almost every word spoken. Josh concluded they were probably reporters from the Edinburgh Evening News, and maybe The Scotsman.

Three court officials were seated in a row ahead of the sheriff's elevated platform, and four lawyers faced them. The lawyers sat immediately in front of the dock where Josh now stood, with his hands clasped behind his back. To his left a burly court guard stood within arm's reach.

The jury bench further along on the right was deserted. The case was deemed suitable for the sheriff alone to pass judgment.

"Mr Robertson, you were the instigator, the director, of the events about which this court has heard," the sheriff continued. "You were the one who took a vehicle without permission. You were the one who escaped lawful custody. For those offences I sentence you to six months in prison, with a minimum of three to be served before parole can be considered." The sheriff banged his gavel. The case was over.

≈

Three days later Suzy was also at the prison, sitting in the waiting room.

"When dis visiting hour finish?" she asked.

Maxine was beside her and checked her watch. "Soon."

"Who'd you think is in there?"

Maxine sighed. "We've already been through the likely suspects."

"Aye, but it's definitely no any of the Gannet crowd. No during prime opening time."

They sat and stared at the muted blue of the wall in front of them. There were two other visitors in the waiting room, an elderly woman and a younger man who were both at the far end of the room where two prison guards stood in quiet conversation.

"I'll book an appointment next time," sarcasm laced Suzy's words. She stared at the far end of the room, willing the door to open. It did. A woman hurriedly stepped through the waiting area, putting on her coat, oblivious to Suzy and Maxine. It was Katrina.

"Whit's she doing here?" Suzy jumped from her seat, Maxine was a split-second behind and pulled her friend back, restraining her momentarily.

Almost as quickly as she had appeared Katrina was gone, exiting through the main door a few steps from where she had entered from an adjacent door. She had not noticed Suzy.

Maxine released her grip on the hood of Suzy's coat. Suzy swung around to face her. "I'm a fool. So I am. How could I be so stupid to think they wouldnae get back together." Her eyes welled up. Maxine threw her arms around her.

"Next visitor for Robertson," called one of the prison guards at the far end.

Suzy pulled away from Maxine's hug, her eyes were red. "I cannae do this," she said, wiping the tears. In one sudden move she turned and marched towards the door that Katrina had moments before exited. Maxine hurried after her, pausing at the door as she watched Suzy break into a jog down the long corridor.

"Next for Robertson," repeated the guard, standing in front of the door that led to the visiting hall. Maxine stood a few feet away. Indecision fogged her mind. Should she chase after Suzy or respond to the guard? She half turned and looked at the prison officer. "Yes, that's me."

Josh was seated at a table in the small hall that was filled with tables where prisoners and visitors sat chatting in huddles. He hadn't been expecting to see Maxine. His eyes widened as she walked through the hall.

"Where's Suzy?" he asked as she sat down opposite him at the table.

"She saw your friend leaving," Maxine was blunt. She stared at him. "What's the story?"

"Story? There isn't any story."

She studied his face.

"There's nae story," he repeated. "She's an old school pal. We're at different places in our lives now. That's it." He waited for Maxine to respond. Her scolding expression remained unchanged.

"Where's Suzy? Bring her in. There's things I need tae say to her."

"What things?" Maxine coldly asked.

"Things."

"Well, she's gone."

A bell sounded and a large prison warden announced visiting time was over.

"Well that was short and sweet," said Maxine. Chair legs scraped backwards on the tiled floor as visitors stood and prepared to leave. Maxine was one of the first to her feet. Josh remained seated, following the protocol for prisoners.

"Is she still staying wi you?" he asked.

"Aye."

"Whit's your address?" Josh asked. "I'll write."

Maxine stifled a laugh. "You'll write! Aye, that'll be the day." Despite her reply, she rummaged through her handbag and pulled out a small notebook and pen. An address was scribbled down and the page ripped out and handed over. But before Josh was able to take it a bald-headed guard, one of several monitoring the room, stretched out an arm and took the paper. He scrutinised the offering.

"It's just an address," Maxine explained.

The guard flicked the scrap of paper over to check both sides. Satisfied it was not an illegal transfer he passed it to Josh, not deeming him worthy of a glance, instead his squinty eyes were fixed on Maxine.

"Visiting time's over," he said. Maxine nodded, took one last look at Josh, and walked away. Josh watched her join the other visitors in a line heading out of the door. He folded the paper and put it into his trouser pocket.

CHAPTER TWENTY

TODAY

The scraping had begun. It was the middle of the night and across the hard concrete floor of the prison cell a piece of furniture was being dragged, inch-by-inch, scrape-by-scrape.

For the past four hours there had been silence, yet sleep had eluded Josh as he battled his restless mind. Lying on a single bed, facing the blank wall, he tried to ignore the scraping. But then the heavy breathing behind him became deeper and more laboured. He could take it no more. He flung off his single blanket and rolled over to face the scraper.

"Give it a rest, will yi!" It was a loud whisper.

"Sorry, I was trying to be quiet," Mal apologised. The scraping stopped.

"Could've fooled me." In the semi-darkness Josh could just make out the silhouette of Mal. He was a short, overweight man, and he had been his cellmate for the past three months. He stood in the darkness wiping sweat from his brow and leaning against the table he was trying to push across the small room. The cell was barely 15ft long by 10ft wide. There were two single, iron-framed beds against opposing walls. The table normally lived at the foot of Mal's bed, but now it was being shoved along the gap between the beds.

"I want to take a look outside," said Mal. The explanation was unnecessary. At least three times a week he had the same urge to look out on the world in the dead of night. The narrow rectangular window was too high up the wall to reach without standing on something.

"You'll get smacked down for this," Josh warned. Moving furniture in the cells was a punishable offence. Privileges would be withdrawn.

"I'll live without my hour in the exercise yard," Mal replied, and resumed pushing the table, scraping it forward. Within seconds he was out of breath again. He stopped. "Give us a hand."

Josh groaned as he rolled out of bed and took hold of one end of the table, while Mal lifted the other just high enough so it no longer dragged against the floor. They carried it to the wall and placed it below the window. Mal climbed up and steadied himself before peering out of the tiny aperture.

Josh flopped back onto his bed and stared at the wall. Normally he slept soundly, unless awoken by the noise of Mal shifting the table. But tonight his cellmate was not to blame for his sleep deprivation; his mind was in overdrive and he'd been awake long before the noise had started. He closed his eyes and tried again. A tantalising drowsiness toyed with his senses but refused to let him drift off. Another hour passed and he heard Mal clambering down from the table, his need to see the nighttime view of the outside world fulfilled.

He waited until Mal was back under his blanket and then got up and climbed onto the table.

"What are you doing?" Mal's voice drifted up from the darkness.

"Looking outside."

"What for? You'll be free in a few hours. No like me, I've got another 11 months," Mal huffed.

"You sound bitter."

"Funny you should say that," Mal rolled onto his side and stared at the wall then closed his eyes.

Josh silently peered out of the window. The distant city streetlights and dark buildings of sleeping Edinburgh were all he could see. He squinted to see further. Barely visible on the far horizon were the three cantilever humps of the immense Forth Bridge. He couldn't see the lonely stretch of Cramond beach, but he knew it was out there, hidden from view, watched over by the bridge. That was where it had started, the genesis for the events that had culminated in his incarceration. The price he had paid was the loss of his freedom and months cooked up in the claustrophobic confines of a prison cell. He wondered if that was all it had cost him. The answer was out there beyond the prison walls, in the darkened streets of the city, and on the beach and under the bridge where the cold waters of the Firth of Forth flowed. He tapped his fingers on the windowsill as he gazed at the distant bridge. In a few hours' time he would be free. Then he would find out.

CHAPTER TWENTY-ONE

FREEDOM

'Dolphin thief jailed' read the bold headline. Suzy scanned the months-old newspaper clipping, folded it and slid it quietly between two books on the bedside table. She lay a little longer in bed, staring at the blank whiteness of the ceiling. The muted noise of an Edinburgh street drifted in from the closed window.

"Are you going to meet him when he comes oot?"

She heard the question, but did not answer immediately. Instead, she closed her eyes and listened to the murmur of the city beyond the bedroom's four walls.

"Did you hear me?" Maxine repeated, entering the room.

"No," said Suzy, her eyes still closed.

"I said are you…"

"No," Suzy interrupted. "No, I'm not going."

Maxine pulled the curtains open. The room was bathed in grey-tinged daylight. From the high vantage point of the third-floor flat she looked down at the city street below, watching people walking along the pavements. A procession of cars and a number 53 double-decker bus snaked along the road. Lifting her eyes skyward she contemplated the clouds and wondered if it might rain before noon.

"What will he think when he doesn't see you waiting at the gate?" Maxine asked.

Suzy opened her eyes and lifted herself up, propping one elbow on the pillow.

"That's up tae him," she replied.

≈

Five miles away Josh was being led through a fourth set of heavy steel-barred doors. He had been counting them. Two prison officers, one either side, were escorting him through the deserted corridors of the jail. Now he stood and waited as one of them secured the latest door and nodded to his colleague to proceed.

"This is the most exercise I've had in months. Might huff tae stop for a wee breather," Josh said. Nobody laughed.

The further he walked, the more doors that clanked shut behind him, the greater the distance he was putting between himself and the stark cell that had been his home for the past three months. There would be no more waking up in the dead of night to the sound of Mal shoving a table across the room.

For Josh the aroma of freedom was a pollen-laden summer breeze coming to greet him. He kept his eyes on the lead guard who was a step ahead. Each time another locked door presented itself the guard reached for the jangling keychain that dangled from his trouser pocket.

Almost free, Josh stood in the holding area before a small cubbyhole hatch, waiting to have his meager possessions returned. A description of each item was read out by a clerk before the items were pushed through the small opening one by one. Josh initialed the paperwork declaring that he had been reunited with the comb, mobile phone, trainers, jeans, duffle coat, holdall bag and £16.23 he had parted with when he had entered the prison.

"See yi again," the clerk said, cracking a wafer thin smile as he took back the clipboard and paperwork.

"I hope no," Josh replied. He put the black duffle coat on and threw his holdall bag, complete with his returned possessions, over his left shoulder. The guard with the keychain led him to a no man's land waiting area. For a moment he was alone in limbo, then a door ahead sprang to mechanised life. As the huge steel portal slowly slid open a shaft of daylight briefly penetrated the prison's grey interior. Josh gingerly hopped outside and took a deep breath. The big door clanked shut behind him. He was free.

It was a back street, fronted by industrial units on one side and the edifice of the prison on the other. Josh glanced along the street and saw a grey car approaching. With his bag slung over his shoulder, he watched as the car slowed. He squinted, trying to see the driver's face. The car picked up speed again as it went past. Josh dropped his bag to the ground.

"Shit. Nae lift then!" He bent to pick up his bag and slung it over his shoulder, before beginning a dejected trudge along the road. It was a long street, and he had almost reached the end when a faded blue car pulled up alongside him.

"And where d'ya think you're going?" called a familiar face from within.

"Stovey, yi bass!" Josh peered through the open passenger window at the driver. "The Gannet. That's where I'm heiding."

"Brill! See you there," Stovey replied and accelerated away just as Josh was reaching for the passenger door.

"Oi, yi bawbag!" Josh shouted. The car sped 50 metres up the road then screeched to a halt. Josh jogged awkwardly towards it, his holdall bouncing off his left shoulder with each step. He poked his head through the open passenger window.

"I was only guising. Get in," Stovey smiled. Josh flung his bag on the back seat.

"See you, pissing aboot," he chided as he got in.

"A'ken, you love it," Stovey replied.

It took fifteen minutes to reach The Gannet. The doors of the pub swung open. Stovey held them ajar as Josh walked in. Applause rang out from one corner of the bar. Angus and Blind Peter were there, and Tom Tom was behind the hatch.

"Look who it is," said Tom Tom, reaching for a clean pint glass. "First one's on the hoose."

The Gannet was about half busy, not bad for a Thursday afternoon, thought Josh. He strolled to the bar, conscious of a few bemused looks from other drinkers who wondered what the commotion was all about.

Angus slapped Josh heartily on the back. "Good to see you again."

Tom Tom pushed a freshly poured pint of heavy across the counter. "So, how was it at the hotel?" he enquired.

"Nothing to write home aboot," Josh replied as he gripped the pint and took a long drink.

"That explains why we didnae even get a postcard," Stovey chipped in. Blind Peter tugged at the front of his string vest and leaned in to hear more.

"It wis all right for youse, getting off scot free." Josh said, wiping his lips as he put down his pint, which was already half empty. "I dae the time and youse lot just stay here in the bar, nice and toasty."

"Well, the sheriff did say you were the ringleader. And it widnae be polite to argue with the sheriff," said Blind Peter.

"So we didnae," Stovey grinned as he accepted a pint from Tom Tom.

"Aye, ma heroes," Josh took another swig of his drink.

"Nae problem. Any time," said Stovey.

Angus stroked his beard. "He couldnae really let you off for escaping from custody. That's a bit of a mandatory time inside for that," he said.

"Aye, that wildlife lassie said a lot of good things. Saved us all a lot of bother. But even she couldnae swing that one," said Blind Peter, lifting his empty glass to alert Tom Tom he needed a refill.

"That's right enough," said Angus. "Where is she by the way. Did you stay in touch?"

Josh was three-quarters of the way through his pint now.

"And what about your Suzy?" Blind Peter asked.

"Nowt," Josh answered quickly. "I wis hoping youse could tell me what's been going on."

There was a silence.

"Has Suzy been around?"

Angus and Peter shook their heads. Stovey examined the rapidly diminishing contents of his pint glass.

"Havnae seen her," said Blind Peter.

"Maybe she's waiting for you," offered Angus.

Josh picked up his glass and downed the last dregs. "Aye, maybe. Well, I'd better no hang around here too long, in case she's waiting at hame."

Almost in unison with his friend, Stovey emptied his pint and banged the glass down on the bar top. "But there's always time for one more. Tam Tam, set them up."

Tam Tam took the glasses and began pouring fresh pints.

"Well, just one more. I dinnae want to upset Suzy on ma first day back," said Josh.

When his second pint was finished, Josh stuck to his word. He slung his bag over his shoulder and headed home. There was a bounce in his step as he walked. He came around the final corner and saw the street that he was so accustomed to, with its front gardens overgrown with wild grass and waist-high steel and wire mesh fences that in most places had fallen apart or been vandalised. He was home.

A rusty blue car was parked further along the street. He did not notice it, but the two occupants had their eyes trained on him.

"There he is. Looks like he's been to the Gannet." Suzy's voice was sharp and strained.

Maxine was sat in the driver's seat and looked across at her friend. "I'd say it would be best to leave him to his own devices, like you said you were gonna do this morning. He's no worth it."

Suzy was silent. Her steady gaze never flinched from the figure walking down the street. She opened the car door and hopped out, marching up the street towards him. Maxine hurriedly exited the car and gave chase.

"Suzy, hang on," she called.

Josh was unaware of the commotion. He was at the front door of the house and about to put his key in the latch when he heard Maxine calling out again. He half-turned and saw Suzy coming along the pavement and up the garden path behind him, hair unkempt, face like thunder.

"Suzy. There you are," Josh said, all welcoming like. But there was no mistaking the stern look on Suzy's face. "Oh-oh. You're either going to give me a hug or a kick in the baws."

Suzy stood inches away and stared. The thunder on her face was not about to be broken by outbreaks of sunshine.

"Suzy!" Maxine jogged into sight at the garden gate. Josh shifted his focus to see her approaching. It was a big mistake. A ringing slap stung his left cheek and almost knocked him sideways.

"That's the end," Suzy stated. Josh raised a hand to protect his cheek from a second hit. None came. He looked uncomprehendingly at Suzy. Hurt filled her eyes along with nebulous tears that she would not allow him the pleasure of witnessing. She spun around and marched from the garden, pushing her way past Maxine at the gate.

"Come on Maxi, you're right, he's no worth it," she said as she walked back to the parked car. The tears she had held back were now in full flow.

Maxine hesitated at the gate before walking up to Josh.

"You really screwed up." She slapped his left cheek a good one. Josh recoiled again.

"Jeez, what is this, beat up Josh day or summit?" he said. "What did I do?"

"It's no what you did. It's what you didnae do."

"Whit? Care to gee us a clue?" he asked.

"You ken. You said you'd write to her."

"Aye, and ..." he started to protest.

"Wheesht," Maxine instructed as she rummaged in her coat pocket and pulled out a square of paper.

"The first day when there was no letter, she drew a teardrop on a piece of paper. The next day she did another, and then another," she said as she unfolded the paper to its full size and handed it to Josh. It was covered in artistically drawn teardrops. Josh studied it as Maxine unfolded a second sheet; it had more teardrops, all identical and neatly drawn in rows.

"I'll save you the bother of counting them up. There's 88," Maxine said.

"Come on Maxi. Dinnae bother with him!" Suzy shouted from further along the street, where she stood next to the car.

"I wrote. I did. I wrote to the address you gave me," Josh defended himself. Maxine looked at him witheringly, then turned and walked away.

"I swear I did," Josh protested.

"Don't listen to him, Maxi," Suzy warned loudly. She didn't need to. Maxine wasn't listening to Josh. She was focused on getting back to her car and getting herself and Suzy as far away as possible from Josh and the crummy housing estate.

Josh stood on the pavement outside the house and watched as Maxine joined Suzy and started the car and drove it towards him before screeching to a halt. Suzy had her passenger window open. Her arm was extended and she held out two keys on a keyring. She let them clatter to the ground.

"I dinnae need them anymore," she said.

The engine revved and the car accelerated away. Josh watched it vanish from sight around a corner. He bent to pick up the keys. There was a screech of bicycle brakes. He looked up to see Gary, the shorthaired bicycle boy, staring down at him.

"Hoo's your face?" grinning Gary asked.

"Whit's it tae do with you?" Josh replied, regaining his full height.

"Your cheek's nice and red. Can I huv a go?"

"I'll tell you what I'll gee you," Josh stepped forward. Gary pulled away on his bike, popping a wheelie. "Slaptastic!" he shouted as he raced down the empty street.

Josh retreated back down the garden path to the house and let himself in. Inside it was cold and dim, permeated by musty, stagnant air, the unloved fragrance of a semi-abandoned abode. Closing the front door he stood in the hallway and listened to the silence. He glanced down at a sprawl of unopened mail and junk flyers on the mat before continuing his slow walk to the kitchen. The kettle was reacquainted with the most favoured burner ring on top of the stove. In the cupboard above the worktop he took out his mug, lingering momentarily as he looked at the mug beside it, with Suzy's name written large across its side. He closed the cupboard door again and waited for the kettle to boil.

As Josh contemplated his mixed-up thoughts, so Suzy was contemplating her own.

She had not said a word for the entire journey back. It was only when Maxine parked the car outside the apartment block that she stirred from her trance-like state.

"You okay?" Maxine asked, brushing some loose hair away from the side of Suzy's face. Suzy smiled back weakly and got out of the car. Maxine grabbed her handbag from under her seat and opened the car door, then stopped. A nagging thought refused to be stilled. She rummaged through the contents of the bag and pulled out a small notebook, flicking through its pages. Then she froze.

"Shit," she cursed.

Suzy walked around the car and stood by the open door.

"What is it?" she asked.

CHAPTER TWENTY-TWO

LOST AND FOUND

"It's vacant." Maxine peered through the window of the ground floor flat. Inside was a sparse, two-bedroom apartment devoid of furniture and all signs of habitation. The layout was identical to her own flat two floors up, and judging by the coating of dust and dirt on the window it had been unoccupied for some time.

Suzy stood beside her. She was holding the pocket notebook from Maxine's bag and looked again at the stub of the torn page, running a finger along the frayed edge where the only mark was a hastily scribbled number one, the bottom part of which was missing – lost when the page had been ripped out.

"There must be some of the number one on the other piece," she said.

"Maybe, but not much," Maxine responded as she turned from the window. "I wrote 12, but when I ripped the page it might have looked like just a two. And if it did, then…"

"Then, maybe he did write," Suzy filled in, handing the notebook back. "I'm no convinced."

Maxine nodded. "There's one way to find out. Come on."

A cordless drill was retrieved from Maxine's top floor flat. She carefully placed it against the key lock of mailbox two, one of 16 in the mailbox nest that was just inside the main door entrance of the building. The drill whirled and cut into the lock mechanism. A cacophony of metal screeching against metal reverberated down the corridor of the flats complex. It didn't take long for one of the ground floor residents to poke his nose out to find out what was causing the racket. He was a tall man, of retirement age, with thinning white hair. He stood at the door of flat number one and glared. Maxine continued drilling.

"It's okay. She's lost her key. We're going to replace the lock," Suzy blustered, doing her best to block the view so he would not see which mailbox was being forced. "It'll only take a minute."

The elderly man shook his head, disgruntled and retreated into his flat. There was a metallic thud and Maxine stopped the drill, pulling it from the hole where the key lock barrel had fallen from view inside. She opened the box and reached inside, pulling out five letters. Three were addressed to the previous occupant. Maxine handed over the other two. Suzy stared at them. They were addressed to her in handwriting she immediately recognised as Josh's.

The pair returned to Maxine's top floor flat where the muffled sounds of the outside world were barely audible inside. Maxine had made tea and now stood at the lounge window, cradling a cup and gazing down at the congested street below. A car horn blew twice. She turned and looked back at Suzy who was sitting in one of the two armchairs, holding the second of the letters. She would sporadically read aloud a passage. She was in another of her silent reading moments. Maxine examined her friend's face, but found it impossible to determine her feelings. Then Suzy spoke again.

"I will continue to write. My future letters I will send to our home, the place where we both belong. Love you forever," she said.

"I never realised he could write like that. And two letters," Maxine observed. Suzy said nothing, but scanned the writing again and allowed the words to sink in.

"He says he'd write to me at Bain - when I moved back in," Suzy paraphrased.

"And dae you think he did?" Maxine asked.

Suzy stood up. She gathered Maxine's car keys from the coffee table.

"I need to go back."

"I'll drive," said Maxine, quickly putting her cup on the table.

"No. I need to go alone," said Suzy, who was already halfway to the door.

The words Josh had written filled her mind, tumbling and scattering with her own jumbled thoughts as she drove through the city streets in the growing darkness. She thought of the years they had spent together and the loving moments shared. Even the arguments had, in a strange way, brought a deeper connection between them. Had she misjudged him? Had she shut herself off? Questions bumped and careered.

She turned the car off the main road and into the housing scheme, guiding it to a parking space on the opposite side of the road a few houses down from the one she and Josh had shared. She could see the living room lights at the front of the house were on. He was in. She switched off the engine and sat for a moment, composing her thoughts, pulling out the two letters and rereading them again in the glow of the streetlights. She took a deep breath and opened the door, but as she did she heard Josh's voice talking to someone outside the house. She hopped back into the car, ducking from sight but staying just high enough to peer through the windscreen. At first she could see nothing, then Josh and Katrina appeared. They walked from the garden and strolled to a nearby car.

Suzy's heart sank as she watched them get into the car. The engine started and the lights flicked on, then the car pulled away and drove down the long, straight street. She watched it depart, one moment visible, the next merely a pair of rear lights in the darkness between the orange skirts of illumination cast by the streetlights. Slowly she slid upwards until she was sitting fully in the driver's seat, then she stepped out of the car again and stood in the gloaming of the evening, watching the departing car's distant taillights until they vanished from view.

Still clutching the two letters, she walked across the road and entered the front garden of the house. She paused and looked around, checking to see if she was being observed. But there was no one watching. In neighbouring homes curtains and blinds were drawn against the night; the flickering, luminous light from television screens danced behind them. She momentarily wished she too was ensconced in one of those warm, if predictable, regular households. She hurried down the path, stopping halfway at a small rockery to rummage between the large stones and heather until she found a small buried steel box and the spare door key inside.

Inside the house it was dark and still. She closed the door behind her and made way to the living room where a table lamp had been left switched on. It bathed the room in a creamy half-light. There were two mugs on the coffee table, one with a smudge of lipstick. Both were empty. A mobile phone blinked away next to the lipstick mug.

She slumped onto the sofa. Tears filled her eyes. Her mobile phone rang and she pulled it from her pocket to see Maxine's name illuminated on the display. She switched it off without answering, and allowed her head to slump against her chest.

How long she stayed in that position, she wasn't sure. Time had lost all relevance. All she was aware of was the sofa, the table, and the lonely tears that rolled down her cheeks.

Then there was the sound of a key turning in the front door lock. She jumped at the noise, sitting upright, alert and rubbing the tear streaks from her face. Someone hurriedly entered the house. A figure dashed into the living room. It was Katrina. She grabbed the mobile phone on the table. As she turned to leave she jumped with fright, noticing Suzy sitting quiet and still on the sofa.

"Suzy!" Katrina blurted.

"Aye," Suzy replied, wiping her left cheek again and doing her best to avoid making eye contact.

"I left my phone," Katrina said, apologetically. Suzy nodded, stood up and walked from the sofa to the far side of the room, keeping her back to Katrina in order to hide the torment and hurt that was sweeping through her. There was a moment of uncomfortable silence as Katrina tried to figure out the situation. A car horn outside broke the silence.

"That's him. Isn't it?" said Suzy, without turning. It was a question only in appearance. She knew the answer.

"Yes," Katrina replied. "Look, it's not what you think…"

"Don't worry, I'm leaving. I shouldn't have come back," Suzy interrupted, still looking away at the back patio doors and the night-shrouded garden. "And I'm no blind. I saw you visiting him at the prison."

"What?" Katrina was caught by surprise. "Yes, of course I went to see him. I wanted to tell…"

"How often did you go?" Suzy interrupted.

"Once."

"Yeah, right."

"I went once, just to thank him for what he had done for the dolphin, despite my interventions," Katrina expanded.

Suzy folded her arms as tightly as her overcoat would allow. She remained stony-faced and continued to stare at the patio doors. But she was no longer looking at the black void outside. Instead, she focused on her own reflection, her dark, tear-heavy eyes, her pitiful expression, and then shifted her gaze to the more distant reflection of Katrina still standing by the living room door.

"And I asked him what he had learned from it all," Katrina continued.

"Aye. Care to share?" said Suzy.

"It's best he tells it to you himself."

Slowly shaking her head, Suzy tutted, "That bad, huh?"

"No, not at all. You'd be surprised," replied Katrina.

"I doubt it. But tell me something else. You say you only went to see him once in the jail, and yet here you are visiting him on the day he gets oot. Cannae live without him, I'd say," said Suzy.

"Suzy, it's not like that. I'm not here to rekindle something from our childhood, trust me."

Suzy was silent.

"I wanted him to come and see something, and I want you to come too," Katrina continued.

"What?" Suzy maintained her cool detachment.

"You need to come and see."

There was another silence as Suzy considered the offer. "No," she bluntly replied, finally turning from the window to face Katrina. Her tears had stopped and her face was a mask of defiance. The car horn sounded again.

"He's getting impatient. You better no keep him waiting," she said with a touch of mocking.

"He loves you," said Katrina. When there was no reaction from Suzy she continued, "He said he would write."

"He did," Suzy said, matter-of-factly, her head dropping slightly. Then she stepped forward purposely. "Now if you'll excuse me I've got to get on with the rest of my life."

"Wait," Katrina urged, putting out an arm to halt Suzy's progress, but Suzy shoved it out of the way and continued her march into the hallway, she was almost at the front door when Katrina pulled at her left arm.

"Wait," Katrina repeated.

Suzy countered Katrina's pull, tugging herself free of her grip, but as she did so she lost her balance and stumbled to the floor, her head almost hitting the closed front door. Something soft cushioned her from the hard floor. Katrina reached out with the offer of a hand to help her back up, but Suzy was distracted by what she had landed on.

"Suzy, I'm sorry. I didn't mean that," Katrina apologised then, noticing Suzy's attention was elsewhere, said, "That's what I wanted to tell you about."

Suzy got to her feet unaided, holding the bundle of mail she had landed on.

"They're all from him," Katrina said. "Come, you can read them on the way."

Suzy shook her head slowly as she looked through the letters, nearly all addressed to her. "No. I need to read these first."

The car horn sounded again. Suzy looked Katrina in the eye. "Don't tell him I'm here."

Katrina held up her mobile phone. "You need to come. Call me when you're ready." Suzy did not respond. She moved past Katrina and back into the front room, clutching the jumble of envelopes.

Katrina watched her go then opened the front door and headed back into the night. When she reached her car she hurriedly climbed inside and shut the door.

"Did you make yourself another cuppa?" Josh joked.

"Dinnae," she said abruptly, starting the engine and pulling away from the curbside.

Josh looked at her. "What is it? Did ya…"

"Wheesht," Katrina instructed. "I'll tell you later."

"You'll tell me later. And you're no saying where we're goin' either. Aye, it's a night o' secrets tonight," said Josh.

CHAPTER TWENTY-THREE

FIN

The full moon had painted a silvery pathway across the Forth River. Gentle waves added texture to its wide expanse. In the distance the three spans of the Forth Bridge were shadowy sentinels against the night sky. The sands of Cramond beach had a pale luminance. Josh knew the place well. He'd known it all his life. In the dark of night it held no fear for him. It was an old friend. As he and Katrina walked from the car park onto the moon-glossed sand his thoughts were transported back to younger days, to adventures and great escapes played out on this stretch of beach. The sounds were timeless and unchanged. Waves lapped against the sand, while a gentle jangle chimed like an undercurrent rhythm as pebbles slid over one another in the to and fro of the tide, and there was the soft pad-pad of his and Katrina's feet on the sand.

The melancholic moment was broken by a new sound. It was one Josh recognised – the a cappella refrain from the Suzanne Vega song 'Tom's Diner'. Katrina fumbled for her phone. The ringtone stopped as she answered the caller. Josh carried on walking for a few more steps. Then he paused to take in the panorama of the warm night, the inky black of the sky, the moonlight reflecting on the firth and the distant structure of the Forth Bridge. Further out were the twinkling lights of homes two miles distant on the opposite shore.

Katrina had finished her call. "You stay here. I've got to go back," she said.

"Go back? Again? What did you leave behind this time?" Josh had turned to face her, but she was already preoccupied stowing her phone in her pocket and retracing her steps to the car park.

"Just stay here. I'll no be long," she called as she hurried away.

Josh stood and watched as she left the beach and vanished from sight. He turned back to face the waters of the firth, slowly resuming his lonely walk along the sand. His eyes were again drawn to the silvery ribbon of moonlight on the water. As he looked at it something else caught his attention, a dark shape – a dorsal fin. He hurried to the water's edge. The fin was moving parallel to the shore and staying close, only twenty feet or so from the beach. Then it disappeared beneath the waves. He reached the point where the lapping water touched the edge of his shoes and stared at the place where he had last seen the fin. Then she appeared, her blonde hair wet and silky rising from the waves.

"Dolly," Josh called.

Her head and shoulders were out of the water. Josh stepped forward, entering the Forth. He was quickly thigh-deep with the cold water lapping against his sodden jeans.

"No, stay there, you daftie. You'll get soaked," Dolly instructed, with a giggle. Josh stopped where he was in the shallows.

"You made it then," he said.

Dolly nodded. "Thanks to you, and your friends."

"Aye, a right shower usually, but they have their moments," Josh replied.

Dolly looked at him, tilting her head slightly to the left. Strands of lank, damp hair crossed her forehead, shrouding her left eye.

"Have you been back on the … swally?" she ventured, with the faintest trace of a smile.

"No, I've no been swallying. Just a couple when I got released and then hame," he replied. "Good to see you've learned a few words from me, swally, daftie. No bad."

Dolly smiled. "And what have you learned?"

Josh scratched an imaginary itch on the back of his head as he bought a few seconds of thinking time. "The value of friendship. Friends that stick by you even when things are going tits up."

"Your drinking pals?"

"Aye," he answered. "And you."

Dolly glanced down at the dark water that encircled her, and then back at him. "How did you know you were doing the right thing?"

"Instinct, I guess."

"I guess," Dolly said. There was a pause. She kept her eyes on Josh. "And now?"

"Now what?"

"Those two women that think so much of you." She flashed a smile.

"Who, Suzy and Katrina? I dinnae think so. Katrina has told me as much. We've both grown up. Things change. We're still pals," Josh answered, shifting his weight from one foot to the other. "And Suzy? That blew up a long time ago. The swallying took care of that good and proper. She doesn't want anything to do we me, she didnae even reply to ma letters. Serves me right. I suppose I'm going to have to start looking again…"

Dolly held a finger to her lips. "Listen," she instructed.

Josh fell silent. All he could hear was the gentle lapping of the water against his jeans, and the tide softly caressing the sandy beach in the darkness. "I don't hear anything," he said.

"Sssh, listen. No, really listen." Dolly had taken the finger away from her lips, but was no less insistent. Josh strained to hear any noise beyond that of the lapping water. Gradually he discerned the faintest chime as a breeze threaded through the distant steel framework of the Forth Bridge. He wondered if that was what she wanted him to hear, but he said nothing. Dolly's eyes were fixed on some point in distant space. She was listening. *Really listening.* Josh tried harder, straining for the slightest whisper. Time stood still. He had no idea how long they had been listening. It could have been five minutes or it might have been twenty. The trance-like state was only broken when his teeth started involuntarily chattering. He refocused. Dolly was staring intently at him, her eyes fixed on his.

"Sometimes the one you're searching for is the one who is already standing beside you," she said. Then she was gone, her head and shoulders vanished beneath the surface of the water leaving only a momentary imprint of ripples.

"Wait!" Josh took a step forward and was almost waist deep in the cold water. His eyes darted back and forth, searching, but there was no sign of Dolly.

≈

Alone in the house Suzy had opened the envelopes one by one and read the contents. Some were short scrawled notes about the mundane measure of prison life, while others were much longer and expressed deep thoughts on life and their years-long relationship. Quite a few were little more than a few basic drawings. One had a badly drawn picture of a man holding flowers next to a woman. There were a few words beneath the drawing.

'Nothing much has happened since I wrote yesterday. So here's a picture of me giving you flowers. I've no done this enough.'

Then she had stopped and searched through the date stamps for the most recent posting. She found it, yesterday's date in slightly smudged ink in the top right-hand corner. She had slid a finger beneath the sealed flap on the back and run it along the edge, then she'd read the words on the small piece of paper inside.

'Well, this is it. Ma last day in Her Majesty's Fair Pleased With Herself Hotel. Cannae say I'm overly impressed. Room service is

atrocious. I had to make my bed myself – everyday! As for the view out of the window, nothing that a few daisycutter bombs couldnae improve. And don't get me started on the food. I'm no staying here again. That's a promise!

'I've had time to think about what I've done in life and what I should have done. I've done you wrong, I'm sorry and I'm fair scunnered and embarrassed. My eyes were only truly opened at the end when I saw the faith you put in me. I ken these are only words, but from tomorrow they'll be actions. I haven't heard back from you, I guess you've been taking stock of everything. The morn I'll be a free man again. They're letting me out at 11. It would be extra special if you were there when I 'escape'. Our new life together starts here.'

Now, as she sat in the passenger seat of Katrina's car, Suzy studied the letter again, running her fingers along the words and tracing around the large heart shape drawn at the bottom. With each streetlight the car passed beneath the words sparkled to life then vanished, before reappearing like a beacon of hope as the next streetlight was reached.

Suzy felt the car slowing down and looked up. They were in a small car park. Through the windscreen she saw the headlights cast twin paths of light over the deserted sands of Cramond, then they were extinguished. Katrina pulled the key from the ignition.

Suzy stepped out of the car. "The way I acted earlier, I'm sorry," she said.

"There's no need to apologise. I'd probably have reacted the same," Katrina replied, locking the car. Suzy walked a few steps ahead and adjusted her eyes to the darkness of the beach and the silvery-tinged water beyond. She led the way down a short flight of steps to the beach.

"That day you saw me at the prison," Katrina continued, catching up with Suzy who had now stopped to listen. "Josh and I had a long talk about things, about relationships and the past. We both could see we'd moved on in life. What we had was special, but that was when we were both a lot younger."

Katrina paused to look out over the Firth of Forth with the binoculars she was carrying, searching the miles of dimly lit water.

"I came looking for the boy I remembered. The one who cared enough to protect the things that meant the most to him. The rebel who...."

Her words trailed away, the sentence unfinished. She lowered the binoculars to take in the panorama.

"I found that he'd grown up, become a man. His flaws magnified," she paused. "As well as the goodness in his heart."

Suzy looked away, her eyes were now accustomed to the darkness. Faint shadows emerged, encroaching on the dim grey sand.

"And that he is in love," Katrina continued, gathering back Suzy's attention. "In love with someone who cares about him more than she realises."

Suzy was caught in a moment of reflection, her gaze falling to the sand at her feet.

"Aye," she whispered and turned away to resume her search of the beach. In the mid-distance she spotted a silhouette against the silvery waters.

"For heaven's sake, there he is. What's he doing, trying to catch another dolphin?" she declared, before breaking away into a jog towards the figure in the shallows.

"Get oot of the water, are you off your heid!" she shouted. Katrina watched her go, then raised the binoculars and looked out across the water.

"What are you doing?" Suzy cried out as she approached the edge of the shore. Josh had waded back and was almost out of the water.

"Suzy!" he said, pulling at his soggy, sagging jeans. "I didnae hear from you. I thought you'd given up on ma sorry backside."

"That's why you were going for a midnight dip?"

"No," he looked over Suzy's shoulder at the distant, solitary figure of Katrina further along the beach. "Does she know?"

"Know what?"

"She was here, no long ago. Have you told her?"

Suzy turned her head to look back at Katrina, then faced Josh. "No. And I never got any of your letters."

"What?"

"But I have now."

Josh nodded but said nothing.

"All those things. Did you mean them?"

"Aye."

Suzy rummaged in her coat pocket, pulled out one of the letters and handed it to him. "Including that one?"

Josh unfolded it and read silently, giving voice only to the last sentence. "Our new life together starts here." He refolded it and handed it back.

After a pause, he said, "Especially that one. I've no right even asking." He could feel his body shivering, but he couldn't be sure if it was caused by his semi-immersion in the chill waters of the Forth, or because he felt the vulnerability of naked, emotional honesty. "I ken I've blown it big time. And you deserve someone more...more attentive."

"Like you," Suzy said.

"No," he responded, missing the cue. "No like me. I'm no...."

Exactly as Dolly had done earlier, Suzy placed a finger to her lips and Josh fell silent.

"Attentive," Suzy lowered her finger. "Like you were, to the dolphin's needs. That was attentiveness. Where did that come from?"

Josh avoided her eyes, and looked at the sandy beach. "It was something I'd lost touch with."

Suzy reached out and gently gripped his left arm. "That was the real you."

"So, what happens now?"

"You have to ask?" Suzy raised her eyebrows. Josh shook his head, leaned in and kissed her.

The moment was broken by a cry from further along the beach. It was Katrina. "There!" She was looking out to sea through her binoculars and pointing. Suzy and Josh hurried to her side.

"Dolphins," Katrina said. "Five, no six."

Suzy and Josh had their eyes on the distant point out in the Forth where Katrina gestured. With the moonlight on the water they could see the dark shapes.

"One of them has a small nick on its dorsal fin. She's the one you rescued," Katrina continued.

"Are you sure?" Suzy asked.

"Yes, it has to be. This is why I wanted you to come tonight. We had calls earlier from people who saw this pod from the beach."

"The same day Josh got out," Suzy smiled at him. "Do you think they knew?"

Josh placed an arm around her shoulders. "One of them, one of them knew," he answered.

Appendix: Dictionary of Scottish and slang words in this book

Aboot – about

Afore – before

Ain – own

Any'hing – anything

Aye – yes

Bampot – foolish / stupid person

Boozer – pub/bar

Buckies – backsides

Cannae – cannot

Couldnae – could not

Dae / Daein – do / doing

Daftie – foolish person

Dalfin – dolphin

Deed – dead

Didnae – did not

Dinnae – do not

Dis / Disnae – does not

Doon – down

Dunno – don't know

Fae – from

Faither – father

Fallow - follow

Feart – afraid

Fur – for

Fuzz – police

Gaunae – going to

Gie / Gied – give / given

Gob – mouth

Guisers – jokers

Guising – messing around

Hame – home

Heid – head

Hoo – how

Hoose – house

Huv – have

Havenae – have not

Innit – isn't it

Isnae – is not

Ja'fancy – do you fancy

Jist – just

Ken – know

Ma – my

Mare – more

Nae / Nah – no

Nowt – nothing

Oor – our

Oot / Oootside – out / outside

Polis – police

Roond – round

Shouldnae – should not

Summit – something

Swally / Swallying – drink / drinking [alcohol]

Toon – town

Waater – water

Wan – one

Wheesht – be quiet

Whit – what

Wi – with

Wis – was

Wisnae – was not

Wouldnae – would not

Wrang – wrong

Yi / Yir – you / your

Yin - one

Youse - you

ABOUT THE AUTHOR

Scott Neil is a writer and journalist. He grew up in Scotland and England and has travelled the world, living in Australia, United States, Russia and Bermuda.

For more than 25 years he has worked on newspapers in the UK and Bermuda. He is a keen roadrunner, and in his spare time also plays guitar, reads and catches up on movies.

He loves to escape to places of wilderness to appreciate nature and the wonders of the world.

His other books are

EATING CLOUDS (2008)
LENNON BERMUDA (2012)

Stories and poems also appeared in the young writers' collection
INSPIRED (1987)

If you have enjoyed this book, please consider leaving a review at Amazon - even if it is only a line or two. Word-of-mouth is crucial for any author to succeed.

Scott talks about his writing and other things he finds of interest, on his website and blog. If you would like to receive an automatic email when his next book is released please visit the website and sign up to receive the special advance notification.

www.scottneilauthor.com